Laon in the School of the Gladiators.

See page 63

GLAUCIA.

A STORY OF

ATHENS IN THE FIRST CENTURY.

By EMMA LESLIE,

AUTHOR OF "DAYBREAK IN ITALY," "CONSTANCIA'S HOUSEHOLD," ETC.

THREE ILLUSTRATIONS.

NEW YORK:
NELSON & PHILLIPS.
CINCINNATI: HITCHCOCK & WALDEN.
SUNDAY-SCHOOL DEPARTMENT.

Entered according to Act of Congress, in the year 1874, by

NELSON & PHILLIPS,

in the Office of the Librarian of Congress at Washington.

PREFACE.

IN the pages of the following tale I have endeavored to show some of the many difficulties with which Christianity had to contend, on its first introduction to the centers of civilization, not only from paganism and philosophy, but from every mode of life and the whole tone of thought then prevailing. It was an age at once of atheism and superstition; of boundless wealth and the most abject poverty; of reckless luxury and selfish cruelty; and against all these, with the long train of evils they bred and fostered, the simple Gospel story of the life of Jesus, as told by a few fishermen, was all this new power could boast.

That it would make any progress in such a world of corrupt, luxurious, cruel pleasure lovers, or proud, self-satisfied, disdainful philosophers, seemed impossible; for what chance had a religion whose whole teaching ranged itself against every thing that the popular mind accounted as worthy of notice? It had no gorgeous ritual, there were no feasts or games in its service, it held out no hope of wealth or power; but, on the contrary, was despised, sneered at, and contemned by the rich and powerful, and yet, in spite of all the abounding corruption on the one hand, and the proud disdain of Jews and philosophers on the other, this "grain of mustard-seed" grew so mightily, that before its first founders had passed away its branches had spread into many lands, and weary souls were resting beneath their shadow.

In "Glaucia" I have endeavored to give a slight sketch of the manners and customs prevailing at this time, introducing a few personages mentioned in the New Testament, as Dionysius of Athens, Phœbe the deaconess of Corinth, and Paul the prisoner at Rome. For the necessary information in preparing this work, I am under deep obligations to Howson and Conybeare's "Life of St. Paul," Stanley's "Sermons and Essays on the Apostolical Age," Kitto's "Bible Cyclopedia," Neander's "Planting of the Christian Church," Mosheim's "History of Christianity," "Gibbon's Rise and Fall of the Roman Empire," as well as other works.

In the remaining volumes of this set of books on Church History I shall endeavor to present the most striking epochs and well-known historical characters in such a way as to link the apostolical age of Paul to that of his successor Luther, thus throwing light upon many dim pages of Church history, and noting the rise and progress of those errors that gradually crept in, so that Rome rivaled paganism in its evil and corruption, until Luther arose, and by his mighty voice awoke slumbering Europe to its need of a reformation.

CONTENTS.

Illustrations.

GLAUCIA.

CHAPTER I.

THE BROTHER AND SISTER.

MORNING sunshine was just gilding the top of the Capitoline Hill, bringing into view the parent temple of the imperial city—the shrine of Jupiter Tonans—but as yet the shadow still lay on the palaces and temples below, and only the first faint bustle of life was heard stirring this heart of the world—this mistress of nations—Rome.

The slight noise that came, borne on the morning breeze, did not arise from temple or palace, but away from these, down among the busy haunts of men, where moved a motley crowd of men, women, and children—Britons, Greeks, and Egyptians, for the most part—whose groans and curses, in different languages, mingled with the crack of the whip and the oaths of their Roman masters; for they were a party of slaves on their way to the market. There was to be a large auction to-day, and so before the rising sun had run its course, brothers and sisters, husbands and wives, might be parted forever.

In the midst of this group walked a boy and girl, clasping each other by the hand, while the tears occasionally fell from their eyes, and they shuddered at the oaths they did understand, although much of what was said was utterly incomprehensible to them. They had been placed near the middle of the crowd, that the driver's lash might not fall upon them, as its marks would be likely to lessen their value, for they were no ordinary slaves. The girl looked delicate, but gave promise of being beautiful; and the boy's lithe, supple, graceful figure spoke of refinement, such as few of the others could boast. They each wore long white linen tunics, which bespoke their nationality, even if the girl's rich golden hair had not told the tale; and there was little fear that any one would mistake the noble Greek outline of the boy as he stooped to whisper some word of encouragement to his little sister.

"Hush, my Glaucia," he whispered; "I am almost a man, and I will work for our freedom; thine first and then my own."

But the prospect of parting with her brother was too near for her to take any comfort from this promise yet.

"If they had only taken us to the slave-market at Athens, Laon, some friend might have bought us together," she sobbed.

"It may be that some one will buy us both now," said the lad; but it was easy to see that the word "buy" almost choked him as he uttered it, and his eyes glowed and flashed defiantly at the thought of his slavery. To Glaucia, however, separation from her brother was all she could think of at present. She knew nothing of slavery, for she had only been taken from a luxurious home a short time before; but Laon was her only friend in the wide world now, and she clung to him with passionate affection.

The slave-market was reached at last, and the poor creatures were ranged in groups, according to their value, and seated under the porticoes ready for the inspection of purchasers; but the two young Greeks were seated by themselves, and Glaucia was directed to smooth her tumbled hair, and Laon to look less angry and defiant.

"But I feel angry and defiant," said the boy; "thy laws are unjust to allow the Roman creditor of my father to sell us for his debt."

The man, who was arranging the different groups, merely shrugged his shoulders. "It were well for thee not to question our laws," he said, "but make thyself as happy as thou canst."

"Happy!" repeated Laon; "can a *slave* ever be happy?" and he dashed away the tears that, in spite of all his efforts, would come welling up to his eyes.

It was now Glaucia's turn to try and comfort her brother, and as the sunlight came stealing into the market-place, and a gentle breeze from the Tiber lifted her golden hair, she said, "See, Laon, our goddess Athene hath not forgotten us here in Rome, and it may be she will still let us be together."

But Laon shook his head sadly, and replied, "Athene is angry with us, Glaucia, and is punishing us for what happened years and years ago, soon after thou wert born."

"What was it?" asked Glaucia. "What could have made our goddess angry with us? Was not our father one of the noblest Epicureans in Athens?"

"He was accounted one of the richest," said Laon.

"Then he must have been a favorite with the gods," said Glaucia.

"Then, dost thou not see, little sister, that as only the rich are the favorites of the gods we cannot be, for we are poor," said Laon.

"But—but thou saidst something had happened, Laon—something that hath made our

Athene angry with us. Tell me, what is it?" she added coaxingly.

But Laon shook his head. "Nay, I know not what it is myself," he said; "but our old nurse told me before we left Athens that our mother was not dead, as we had always supposed, but had offended Athene."

"*Our* mother," repeated Glaucia, "was she kind to us as our brother Apecides' mother was to him? O, Laon, where is she? for we should not be sold to pay our father's debts if we could only find her."

But Laon only shook his head. "I know nothing but what our nurse told me, but I mean to find out all about it when I am a man."

Glaucia looked at her brother, and then at the tall Roman soldier who came lounging through the market at this moment, as if measuring them mentally.

"It will be a long time before thou art a man," she said.

"I am a man now," said Laon seriously. "I am only sixteen, and was a boy a month since, but I shall never be a boy again, Glaucia. Thinking of thee and my mother, and how she offended all the gods of Athens, has changed me, and I want to do a man's work in the world —to free thee and find my mother, if she lives."

"O, Laon, if we were only free we would go back to Athens and begin our search. Hast thou any clew?" she suddenly asked.

Laon reddened and put his hand to his breast, and then, after some hesitation, drew forth two small rolls of parchment.

"I have these," he said, "one for thee and one for me; our nurse Lepida gave them to me, and they were left in her charge by our mother."

"O, Laon, let me see," said Glaucia, as he slowly unrolled one of the slips. They looked at the writing together, but neither being able to read they could make nothing of it. "I wish I could understand it," continued Glaucia. "I will learn to read, if I can."

In a moment the parchment was snatched from her hand, and Laon's face worked convulsively as he said,

"Glaucia, thou shalt not—must not! No Greek maiden of virtue ever learns that which would at once defame her. Didst thou never hear why my father would not let me learn any thing—why he grew to hate learning so much?"

Glaucia opened her eyes in wondering amazement. Laon was always so gentle with her, but now he spoke so passionately that his frame trembled, and he looked as though he were about to destroy her precious manuscript.

"What is it—what is the matter?" she asked.

"Glaucia, our mother wrote this," said Laon slowly and impressively.

But Glaucia did not seem to be greatly surprised, and merely said,

"I wish I had learned to use the stylus."

"Athene preserve thee from such a fate!" said Laon devoutly. "Glaucia, if I fulfill my mother's wish and give thee one of these, mind, thou must keep it a secret that *our* mother ever used the stylus—ever wrote these words, whatever they may be."

"But thou, Laon, will learn to read, wilt thou not?" asked Glaucia; "thou wilt want to know what our mother says to us here."

Laon colored and hesitated for a minute or two, but at length he said,

"Learning is good for a man, but for a woman it is a shame and disgrace."

"And was it through this that our mother offended Pallas Athene?" asked Glaucia.

"Through that and something else," replied Laon moodily; "what the other cause was Lepida would not tell me; but—but—but, Glaucia, forget thou ever had a mother," he added quickly.

The girl shook her head.

"I cannot, Laon," she said; "that thou hast told me I can never forget, and when I am a woman I will take this parchment in my hand and go through the world in search of my mother."

"I would that I had forgotten to tell thee this, or that Lepida had not charged me so strictly to do so before we were parted," said the boy.

This allusion to their coming separation brought the tears to Glaucia's eyes again, but their owner coming up at this moment she was told to dry them quickly, as it might prevent his making so good a bargain. He had brought a customer with him, a young Roman patrician, who wanted a Greek dancing-girl to supply the place of one who had died. Laon's eyes flashed fire as he heard this.

"My sister has never learned to dance, most noble Roman," he said boldly.

The gay young Roman looked at Laon, but merely murmured, "Impudence!" as he passed on. His master, however, grew furious with passion.

"Is this the proper behavior for a slave?" he demanded. "Have I not lost enough by thy shameless spendthrift father? Ten thousand sesterces would not pay me for all the trouble I have been at, and now thou wilt cheat me by making thyself of as little value as possible."

"My sister cannot dance," said Laon, "and she shall not be sold for a dancing-girl."

"Ha! sayest thou so, thou miserable Greek slave!" exclaimed the man, striking Laon as he spoke. "I say she shall be a dancing-girl, for I will have her taught that she may—"

But here he was interrupted by receiving a blow from Laon that almost stunned him for a moment. He quickly recovered himself, however, and dragging the boy forward knocked him down, and kicked him as he might have kicked a dog, while Glaucia screamed and begged him to spare her brother, receiving several blows herself as she tried to screen him.

Her screams soon brought a crowd of people together, for the market was fast filling now; but no one interfered when they heard the cause of the uproar.

"A couple of young Greeks have turned upon their master," was the explanation passed from lip to lip, and by the young men it was laughed at as a good joke. To poor Laon, however, it was no laughing matter; for when his master's anger had sufficiently cooled to allow him to leave off kicking he was quite unable to rise, or even to crawl back to his place beside Glaucia, and lay groaning with pain until another slave was ordered to pick him up and carry him to a shed close at hand.

His master cursed himself for his folly in getting into a rage with the boy, for he was quite unsalable now, and might be for some time; while Glaucia had spoiled her good looks for the present, owing to her grief on her brother's account.

She wanted to go with him when he was taken away, and begged very hard to be allowed to do so, for at first her master seemed inclined to relent toward her. The fact was, he was debating the cost of having Glaucia taught dancing; for as a dancing-girl she would be of far more value than a waiting-maid, which was all that she was fit for now; and if he decided to do this, she might make herself useful in trying to cure her brother's wounds.

At length, however, he decided to try the chances of this day's sale, and if he could get a good price for her at once he would take it and rid himself of any further trouble in the matter. So Glaucia was told to go back to her place, and not shed another tear unless she wished to be beaten worse than her brother had been.

"These cursed Epicureans, I will never lend them another sesterce," muttered her master; "they believe in nothing but present enjoyment; and as they think their soul dies with their body, so they seem to think the whole world is coming to an end with them, and if things can only be made smooth for them here, it matters not what happens to others afterward."

Had Laon or his sister uttered this complaint no one could have felt surprised, for their father's misdeeds were being visited most heavily upon them; but Laon could think of nothing now but his poor bruised, bleeding body, and Glaucia was too full of grief and anxiety on her brother's account to think of any thing else. Her mind was so full of this all-absorbing thought that she did not notice the little crowd that gradually gathered round her, until an elderly freedman asked a second time what she was crying about.

Glaucia lifted her head then. "O, my brother! my Laon!" she sobbed; "they have killed him, kicked him to death." But her master coming back at this moment most of the crowd moved away, but the freedman still remained.

"Thou art a slave for sale," he said; and, turning to her master, asked her price.

"A thousand sesterces," said the slavedealer shortly.

"A high price for a waiting-maid," remarked the Roman.

"Too high for thee I doubt not, for, by the helmet of Cesar, thou lookest as though thou didst not possess the half of that sum," said the man in a sneering tone.

The eyes of the Roman flashed angrily. "I came not here to be insulted, but to ask the price of the slave-girl."

"And I have told thee already—a thousand sesterces."

"And I say it is too high; no one will give so much for a waiting-maid."

"Then I will make a dancing-girl of her; she will fetch as much again then," coolly remarked her owner.

"That is true enough, but thou wouldst have to keep her awhile, so that it would not be all profit. Wouldst thou not be willing to get the trouble off thy hands at once for eight hundred sesterces?"

The man shook his head. "The debt she is to be sold for is a heavy one, and I will not take less than the thousand," he said. The man looked at Glaucia again, and asked her several questions. "She is the only Greek girl in the market this morning," he remarked.

"Yes, that she is, and there is not likely to be another for some days."

"And my mistress leaves Rome to-morrow, and will have a Greek waiting-maid before she goes," said the freedman, fingering the coins he carried in his pouch; "make out thy bill. I will take the girl, though I must say it is a high price to charge for her."

Half an hour afterward Glaucia left the slave-market, weeping bitterly for her brother, and wondering whether they would ever meet again.

CHAPTER II.

THE DESPISED SECT.

GLAUCIA and her guide passed on through the narrow, tortuous streets of the city, crowded now with gay chariots, litters, or silver-harnessed horses, for the poorer streets were soon left behind, and they were in the neighborhood of the Forum, the aristocratic quarter of Rome. The poor girl cried until she was almost exhausted, and deep sobs still shook her slight frame, although her mind had begun to occupy itself upon the important question as to who her owner could be. She had heard at the time of her purchase that she was to be a waiting-maid, but beyond this she knew nothing, and her guide had not once spoken to her since they left the slave-market.

They passed the Forum, and pressed on with the crowd through the vast arch of the Porta Caprera. Beyond the city walls villas and gardens surrounded them on all sides, and at the gate of one of these they at last stopped. A crowd of freedmen and clients, as well as several slaves, were loitering in the vestibule, but they moved aside as Glaucia and her guide entered. As soon as they had reached the atrium she was told to sit down, and a female slave was dispatched to inform her mistress of their arrival.

"My mistress is engaged now," said the girl, but as soon as I am summoned to attend her I will tell her thou hast come back."

"Then I will leave the girl here," said the man. "Thou hadst better rest awhile," he added, turning to Glaucia, and pointing to a cushion lying near.

That poor girl needed no second bidding to rest herself, for the long walk and previous excitement had quite tired her out, and in spite of being in a strange place and anxiety on account of her brother, she very soon fell asleep. Just before she closed her eyes she put her hand into her bosom to make sure she had not lost her precious manuscript, and so fell asleep with it in her hand.

Meanwhile her mistress had heard such a glowing account of Glaucia's beauty and sorrowful looks that, hearing she had fallen asleep in the atrium, she went to look at her as she lay, and while still standing near, one of her friends entered to pay her farewell visit, as they were so soon to leave Rome.

"I have come to look at my new purchase," said the lady. "Valeria has been teasing me for the last month to let her have a Greek slave girl, and so I sent to the market this morning and bought this one."

"She does not look like a slave," remarked the visitor, stooping down and examining her features more closely.

At the same moment Glaucia started and the manuscript fell from her hand at the lady's feet, and she at once picked it up. "What have we here?" she said, carelessly opening it as she spoke. She read a few words, and then handed it to her hostess, watching her countenance as she read it.

"How did the girl get this, I wonder?" exclaimed the lady. "But I need not ask," she added; "the Athenians ever love that which is new and strange, and so doubtless they were as willing to adopt this new deity that appeared in Judea as the Emperor Tiberius himself, who would have added the name of Jesus to the roll of our gods and goddesses, and given him a place in our Pantheon, if the Senate had not remonstrated against such impiety." And, placing the roll of parchment close to Glaucia again the lady turned to her visitor and invited her to enter the peristyle, where the other members of the family were assembled ready to receive visitors and discuss the Roman gossip of the day, especially that concerning the Palatine Palace, and the extravagant and infamous Poppæa, who now occupied the throne of the noble-minded Empress Octavia.

But their visitor knew very little of the doings at court. "How is it, Julia, thou takest so little interest in these things now?" at length asked her hostess when, after several questions, the same answer had been returned.

The lady colored slightly as she answered, "Our handsome emperor is less popular with every one than he used to be," and she turned to admire some beautiful wreaths of flowers lying near.

"Valeria will be pleased that her work is admired, for she is almost as devoted to the service of Flora as my Claudia is to her tendance at the vestal-fire of Rome."

"But it was scarcely Claudia's free choice to become a vestal," remarked the visitor.

The mother's cheek flushed, for she knew it was a piece of family ambition, as well as to get rid of the expense of dowering her two daughters, that the younger had been devoted to the service of the goddess at eight years old. But a turn in the conversation took place now by the entrance of Valeria to resume her work of flower-weaving, for which her mother was not sorry.

"Our friend Julia hath been admiring thy work, my daughter," said her mother.

The girl looked pleased. "I was in the garden gathering flowers soon after sunrise this morning," she said; "no slave's fingers have touched these;" and she held up her flower-wreath as she spoke.

She was a tall, noble looking girl of sixteen, with dark, eager-looking eyes, and a wealth of raven hair that almost reached her waist when unbound from the golden fillet that usually confined it.

Her friend smiled faintly at the earnestness of the girl's manner, and yet it was easy to see that deeper thoughts had been stirred within her as she said, "The simple worship of Flora is certainly less harmful than the gladiatorial shows, and yet—"

"Have you any news concerning the arena? Hath our emperor appeared as a gladiator yet? for, as thou knowest, my health will not allow me to mingle much in the gay world now," interrupted her hostess.

"I have not been to any of the games for some time," replied Julia; "not since the emperor shaved his beard, and, inclosing the hair in a box of gold, dedicated it to Jupiter Capitolinus."

"It is to be hoped our father of gods and men valued the gift more highly than I should, for we mortals are growing tired of his childish vanity."

"Even as he wearies of every one who does not encourage it," said Julia. "Thou askest for news of Poppæa; but though I know not any thing of her doings, I have heard the whisper that the emperor is bent upon the destruction of his former tutor, the noble philosopher, Seneca, even as he murdered his mother, Agrippina."

"And Nero owed his throne to his mother's plotting. Yet he has stained his hands with her blood," said the hostess.

"Yes, Agrippina hath suffered for her crimes at her son's hand, for whom they were committed, and those whose lives alone adorned his corrupt court are leaving Rome. The British princess, Claudia, and her husband, Pudens, are going to Britain, as well as Pomponia Graccina."

"I heard a strange tale the other day concerning Pomponia," interrupted her hostess. "It was whispered that she had given up the worship of the gods of Rome and joined the miserable sect called Christians, that are hiding in some of the lowest parts of the city."

Again came the tell-tale blush into her visitor's cheek, and this time it did not escape notice. "Thou hast heard the same story, I can see, and blush to acknowledge that a Roman matron could so degrade herself."

"There is nothing degrading in the religion of these Christians," said Julia timidly.

"Nothing degrading! when they speak against all the gods of Rome and every other nation—do not even believe in their existence at all. Nay, nay, but they are the pests of society, and how thou canst attempt to defend them, my Julia, I am at a loss to understand."

"Thy judgment of these Christians is unjust, my Romola; they are not the pests of society thou thinkest them. Instead of denying the existence of all gods, they worship the one great God who made heaven and earth, and—"

"And who would set himself above our Jupiter, if he could. Had the God of these Christians been admitted to our Pantheon he would not have been satisfied with any but the highest place," said Romola, angrily interrupting her friend.

The gentle Julia knew not what to say, for on the eve of parting with her friend, it might be forever, she had no wish to quarrel, and yet truth demanded that she should say something now. "I wish I could make thee understand something of these Christians and their religion," she at length said.

"But I do not want to understand or to hear any thing about them; it is like thee, my Julia, to try and defend them for the sake of thy friend Pomponia; thou wouldest do the same for Valeria or Claudia, I know, if any one spoke against their favorite goddesses. But let me give thee a word of advice. I am older and wiser than thou, and believe me, this sect will bring upon themselves great trouble by and by through their arrogance, and to be known as their friend may involve thee in the same difficulty; so be wise in time, and never give any one the opportunity of calling thee a Christian."

"But I am a Christian," said Julia quickly, and as the words left her lips she grew as pale as the marble Venus near which she sat.

"Thou—art—a—Christian!" repeated Romola, drawing aside her robe as though the touching of her friend's garments would contaminate her. She spoke with bated breath almost in a whisper, but Valeria and every one else heard it.

She dropped the wreath she was weaving to

gaze at Julia, who sat with her face buried in her hands, trembling almost as much as the mimosa leaves in the porphyry urn close by.

"A Christian!" repeated the girl; "those evil people are only fit to fight with wild beasts in the arena."

No one else spoke for several minutes, and the rustle of the leaves growing in the hanging baskets between the marble columns could be heard in the dread silence that followed Julia's confession. At length, however, she conquered her emotion sufficiently to say, "Thou wilt hold this confession a secret for the present, Romola," as she rose to take her departure.

Her hostess bowed but did not reply, and Julia left the peristyle in silence. As she reached the curtain at the entrance she paused for a moment, and then, turning toward her friends, said, in a firm, gentle voice, "May the Lord Christ bless thee, Romola, and thy children with thee!" and she passed on toward her litter, which was waiting outside.

In the atrium, however, she was overtaken by her friend. The love between them had been very strong, and could not be killed in an instant, although Romola still shrunk from any contact with her visitor.

"One moment, Julia," she said, pausing near

the center where stood the images of the household gods, the Lares and Penates, and glancing at them she forbore to advance a step further, although her visitor was near the opposite entrance and the slave in attendance had drawn aside the curtain: "As thou knowest, we leave Rome for Athens to-morrow, and it may be that trouble will come to thee by and by. If it should be so, and thou needest a refuge, thou mayest be sure of my protection," said the lady, and without waiting to see the effect of her words upon Julia she returned to the peristyle. Her visit to the atrium had brought to her mind what she had almost forgotten in her conversation with Julia, the arrival of her daughter's slave; but seeing Glaucia was awake, she sent for her as soon as she reached the peristyle.

"Now, Valeria, this is thy maid, and I hope thou wilt be satisfied with her," said the lady rather testily, for the occurrence of the morning had somewhat ruffled her temper.

Valeria looked up from her flowers, and beckoned the slave to bring her nearer. "Canst thou weave flower-wreaths for Flora?" she asked.

"I have woven them for Pallas Athene," replied Glaucia.

"Dost thou worship Pallas Athene?" asked the elder lady.

Glaucia looked as though she did not understand the question.

"Athene is the goddess of Athens, the great goddess of light, and wisdom, and knowledge," she said.

"And thou worshiped her when thou wast in Athens?" asked her mistress.

"Yes, and I worship her in Rome, too," said Glaucia.

"But thou hadst a roll of parchment in thy hand to-day; where didst thou get it?"

"My brother gave it me," and at the mention of her brother Glaucia burst into a passionate flood of tears.

The elder lady frowned as she said, "Girl, thou forgettest thou art a slave."

Glaucia had forgotten it for a moment, but she choked back her tears now and tried to restrain her sobs as she said,

"I shall never see my brother again."

"Perhaps not," coolly remarked the lady; "but tell me about this manuscript now. Hast thou read it?"

Glaucia shook her head.

"I cannot read," she said.

"Then thou knowest nothing of the writing,"

said the lady, "and the parchment had better be destroyed."

But Glaucia seized it in a moment.

"O no, no!" she said, tears again rolling down her cheeks, "my brother gave it to me and I must keep it; do, pray do let me keep it," she added.

"Yes, let her keep it, my mother," interposed Valeria at this moment; "she is my slave, as thou knowest, and I will take care that no one else shall see this keepsake. It is for slaves, I suppose," she added, "and would make them dissatisfied if they only read it."

The elder lady was annoyed, but being too indolent to contest the point with her daughter, Glaucia was allowed to keep her precious manuscript, and it being time for the second daily bath, she was handed over to the care of a slave, who was to instruct her how to prepare the unguents and powders used by her young mistress, as well as in the general duties of a lady's-maid.

A few hours later in the day Claudia, the vestal, came to wish her parents and sister farewell, for their stay in Athens might be for many years, and so it was uncertain when or how they would meet again.

The meeting between the sisters was a very

affectionate one, for Valeria looked up with reverence to her sister, although she was younger, for the life of a vestal was considered the noblest and holiest to which a woman could aspire, and the sacred six were chosen from the oldest and purest patrician families in Rome. Highest among these were the Gracchi; a fact never forgotten by either Romola or her two daughters; for to the vestal the honor of her family was as dear and sacred as the shrine she served, and to Valeria no less so, although she looked upon her father's study and love of philosophy as being almost as sacred.

Fabrizzio Gracchi aspired to be a philosopher, and that was why the family were now leaving Rome, for Athens was to him greater than even Rome itself—as much greater as mind and thought are to mere brute strength and force of arms; for these different arenas of power, both now contending for the mastery of the world, did the rival cities represent. Athens ruled the world of mind and thought, as Rome ruled the outer world by force of arms.

To study in the Academy, and walk beneath the shadow of the plane-trees, where Plato and Socrates wrote and mused and Demosthenes uttered his soul-stirring words, was the ambition of many a Roman mind just now; and all the traditions of the past in which his family had been connected with the advancement of the imperial city could not keep Fabrizzio from gratifying his longing to go to Athens. His younger daughter, the vestal, looked upon this as an insult to Rome and a slight to her gods, and to her sister Valeria she confided this feeling before she left.

"Let Greece keep her philosophers, and Rome her heroes," she said; "but let not the heroes seek to be philosophers, or the gods will be offended and our name disgraced."

"Our noble father will never disgrace the name of the Gracchi!" said Valeria warmly.

Her sister looked doubtful—"I am glad I am a vestal and devoted to the service of our Rome—to keep her hearth-fire burning when others are forsaking her. For the sake of our family too I am glad, for which of our ancestors ever forsook the gods or the heroes of Rome?"

In vain Valeria protested that her father was not likely to forsake either. The vestal shook her head. "The defection has begun, and who can tell what the end may be;" and still lamenting this, she returned to her duties at the temple, leaving Valeria vaguely unhappy, for she looked upon her sister's words as oracles that must be fulfilled.

CHAPTER III.

ATHENS.

A VESSEL had been chartered to convey Fabrizzio Gracchi and his family to Athens; and when, after many days' sailing, they at length came within sight of the numerous islands of the archipelago the spirits of the whole party revived, and Glaucia was eagerly asked by her fellow-slaves whether they were within sight of Athens.

"No, we shall see the temple of Pallas Athene first," answered Glaucia; "it stands on the height of Sunium, that sea and land alike may share the goodness of our goddess in her gift of light."

"But there is a statue of Minerva on the Acropolis that the sailors may worship without entering her temple," said Valeria, who was standing near.

"Minerva!" repeated Glaucia. "The Athenians worship Athene, not Minerva."

Her mistress smiled at her ignorance. "We Romans worship the Athene under the name of Minerva," she said. "Flora, the goddess of kindness and beneficence as well as flowers, and Minerva, the goddess of knowledge, are my favorite deities."

Glaucia looked pleased. "Knowledge is good," she said, "at least for men; but for women it is only evil, Laon told me."

She ventured to mention her brother's name to her young mistress occasionally, and Valeria allowed her to do it as a sort of reward for her industry and attention to her varied wants. Glaucia had striven hard to learn the duties of her new station, although it had been any thing but easy to conform to the condition of a slave, and but for Valeria's kindness and consideration would have been almost intolerable. Deprived of her usual occupation of preparing votive offerings for her favorite deity, Valeria had been glad to talk to her little Greek waiting-maid sometimes, and their conversation had generally been upon Athens; and so they now stood together at the prow of the vessel watching for the first glimpse of the temple and far-famed statue of the Acropolis.

Glaucia burst into tears when she caught sight of the helmeted goddess, with her glittering brazen spear, towering above all the surrounding temples, columns and statues, and attracting every eye by its glowing brightness.

"It is gold!" exclaimed Valeria when she saw it.

But Glaucia shook her head. "It is more precious than gold, Laon says, for it is made out of the spears and shields our heroes took at the battle of Marathon."

At last the landing was reached—the Piræus, with its warehouses and covered porches, the all-dominant eagles of Rome floating in the breeze from every flag-staff along the shore. To walk the solid earth again was a relief to all the wayfarers, but to Glaucia it was more welcome than to any one else, when she reflected that she was in Athens, though even her native land could not be to her what it once was, since Laon was not with her to share it. As they entered the city itself, and Glaucia watched the admiration visible in every face by which she was surrounded, her heart glowed with pride and pleasure.

"Athens is more grand, more beautiful than Rome," whispered Glaucia; and truly they were surrounded with such treasures of art as the world has never since equaled. Statues of Neptune, Jupiter, Ceres, Minerva, Apollo, Mercury, and the Muses met their eyes one after another in quick succession. Porticoes, with battle-pieces painted on their fronts; colossal figures of Conon, Epaminondas, Demosthenes, and other illustrious Athenians, all gems of the sculptor's art, were there in all their beauty and grandeur. "But our Parthenon is the most beautiful of all," she continued, with glowing cheeks, as she turned to her young mistress.

"Yes, I have heard of it," said Valeria; "thou shalt guide me thither to-morrow, and we will together present our votive offerings to Minerva, or Athene, as thou lovest to call her."

Glaucia's eyes slowly filled with tears. "Alas! who will care for the votive offering of a slave," she said. "Our great Athene would be insulted by the worship of such as I am now."

Valeria looked at her little waiting-maid pityingly. "Is there no religion for slaves here in Athens?" she said.

"Which among our gods would accept the devotion of slaves? and yet—and yet I should like to go to the Parthenon once more," said Glaucia earnestly.

"Thou shalt go, Glaucia, and thy offering shall be equal to mine, that the goddess may not be offended," said Valeria impulsively.

The house that had been taken for them at

Athens was not unlike the Roman villas on the banks of the Tiber, for Roman houses were becoming quite the fashion in Athens, as Grecian manners and customs were the rage at Rome; and, choosing a bath and bed-room for herself, Valeria took care that there should be one near her own for Glaucia, instead of sending her to the slaves' apartments, near the atrium, or entrance-hall. She was likewise careful that the statue of Flora, in the frigidarium or indoor garden, should be duly honored immediately upon her arrival, and as there were no suitable flowers in their own garden, which had been somewhat neglected of late, Glaucia was at once sent to the market to buy some.

How often Glaucia had walked in the agora, or market-place, with Laon and her nurse in the happy, by-gone days; but looking back now it seemed years since she had rested beneath those shady porticoes, or ran races with Laon, while their nurse bargained for fruit or flowers, or some articles of daily food. There were the same things ranged in the different booths now—books and parchments on one side, and various luxuries on the other. But the booth that moved Glaucia most deeply was that for the sale of slaves, for it brought back to her mind most vividly that awful morning, when she sat in the slave-market at Rome and saw her brother beaten almost to death. Where was he now? What had happened to him since? Had he recovered from his injuries and been sold into slavery, like herself, and had he found a master as kind as Valeria, or was he still lingering in pain and anguish, with no one to tend him or say a word of comfort to him? If these questions could only be answered—if she could only know what had happened, or be sure that some one cared for her brother still, she thought she should be satisfied.

But who was there to care for a poor slave? The gods would not notice them. Kind and pitiful as Athene might be, she could not stoop to care for the sorrows of the poor. They might share her common gifts of light and air, and whatever scraps of knowledge might fall in their way, but her special favors could only be bestowed on the wealthy and noble.

As she had her basket filled with the costly flowers that were to decorate the shrine of Flora, she echoed her mistress' words with a sigh, "Is there no religion for the poor?" and her words were uttered half aloud—at least loud enough for a venerable-looking man who was passing to hear them, and who, pausing for a moment, said, "Hast thou never heard of the religion that has been specially sent for the poor."

Glaucia lifted her large, sorrowful eyes to the stranger's face. "A religion for slaves!" she uttered; "who would be the God of slaves?"

"God Almighty, and his Son the Lord Christ," said the stranger reverently.

Glaucia had never heard the name of Christ before. "The Lord Christ," she repeated; "is he very great?"

"Yes, greater than any of the gods worshiped in Athens," said the old man.

But Glaucia shook her head. "Thou dost forget our great Jupiter, the father of gods and men, whose statue guards the tribunal of the Pnyx."

"He is greater than Jupiter and kinder than Pallas Athene," said the stranger.

"Where is his statue?" asked the girl. "Shall I find it in the Parthenon or on the Acropolis? Tell me where I shall find it; for if he is the god of slaves I will ask him to befriend my brother, who is a slave too."

"The Lord Christ hath no statue in Athens or at Rome," replied the man; "those who worship him must worship him in spirit and in truth."

They had been standing in the market while

this conversation took place, but, glancing at the sun, Glaucia noticed that she had already been a long time from home, and so, picking up her basket of flowers, she said hastily, "I must not tarry longer now, for these are for the shrine of Flora, which must be decked before sunset."

"If thou art sent on an errand I would not hinder thee, although I would fain tell thee something of the love of the Lord Christ," said the old man.

"I may come to the market to-morrow perhaps, but I cannot stay longer now," said Glaucia; and she hurried away, wondering who this new god could be that the old man had told her of, and half hoping, half believing, she should see his image in the Parthenon, in spite of what the stranger had told her to the contrary.

A family so devoted to the service of Jupiter and the gods as the Gracchi were would not fail to present a splendid offering at the shrine of the principal deity to celebrate their arrival in Athens; and so, early the next morning, a train of oxen, with gilt-tipped horns and decked with garlands of ribbon and flowers, were led by white-robed priests to the place of sacrifice, in presence of the Roman philosopher and his family.

The next day Valeria ordered her litter early

in the morning, and, attended by six of her father's lictors and Glaucia, paid her promised visit to the Parthenon. The rocky crags of the Acropolis, contrasting with the dazzling whiteness of this polished marble temple, heightened the effect of its loveliness; but splendid as was its external appearance, it paled before the exquisite variety of its interior, with its magnificent friezes, and that matchless work of art the statue of Minerva, sculptured by the hand of Phidias, and glittering with gold and ivory.

An overpowering sense of awe bowed the heads and hearts of both the girls as they paused at the entrance of the Parthenon, and for a moment they were equals, but only for a moment, for, with a rush of feeling, Glaucia remembered that she was a slave, and their great goddess Athene, would not stoop to accept the devotion of slaves.

She knelt beside Valeria, and burned the incense with her, but still feeling that it was a vain service—that there was an impassable gulf that never could be bridged between her and the great goddess—that she was a slave, and had nothing to do with all this surpassing beauty by which she was surrounded; and so, instead of feeling happier for her visit, she felt more restless than ever, and the longing grew more intense to know something of the religion for slaves that the old man in the market-place spoke of.

She had looked in vain among the statues of the gods for one of this new deity, but she did not tell her mistress how disappointed she felt at not finding another added to the roll. In fact she had not spoken of her meeting with the old man at all, but she began to wish now for another opportunity of seeing him to hear more of the Lord Christ, who had come to be the God of the poor and the enslaved. But several weeks passed before Glaucia was again sent to the market, for her time was fully occupied, when not in immediate attendance upon her mistress, in assisting to prepare those unguents and perfumes so lavishly used by the Roman ladies of that time. At length, however, Valeria needed something that only Glaucia could be trusted to fetch, and so she was sent.

With a beating heart and anxious gaze among those who crowded the different booths did Glaucia press on, looking for the old man she had seen before. But although she peered under every shady portico she passed, and lingered at the entrance of the slave booth, hoping to see him among them, he did not appear, and at length she was obliged to make her purchase, and, turning her steps homeward, was about to leave the agora, when her attention was drawn to a little crowd near the entrance, and on going nearer she saw the old man she had been in search of mounted on a stone, and speaking in a loud tone to the little crowd before him.

"Fellow-citizens, ye remember the Jew of Tarsus, who came a few years ago and spoke in the agora here, as well as on Mars' Hill. Some who are listening to me now listened to him then, when he came to make known to us the God whom the wisest and best of our philosophers spoke of as the 'Unknown God.' Ye have altars in this our Athens to the great Jehovah, but no one has dared to erect a statue, for he is too great to dwell in any form or any temple made with hands, for he created the heavens and the earth, and all nations and conditions of men dwelling upon it; and as our own poet said, we all are his offspring, although we know it not, and grope for him like children in the dark. Plato and Socrates stretched out weary hands in their search for him; but when the fullness of time had come the Unknown made himself known by his Son, the Lord Christ, who took the nature of a man, and suffered all the griefs and woes of a man, and at last even the death of a slave, that he might declare fully the love God felt for his offspring still, and that after death there was hope of eternal union with him in heaven, and of reunion with our lost but loved ones, whom the grave has hidden from our view, but who will yet rise again to immortal life through the power of Christ, who has redeemed them.

"Paul of Tarsus declared this before the noblest of our citizens, but I can only speak with a faltering tongue of what I learned then, and would fain have you remember still. I am not learned, as many of the Athenians are. I never studied in the schools of either Epicurus or Zeno, and know little of the philosophy that is accounted so great. But I have learned what neither the Stoics nor Epicureans could teach —the love of God shining in the face of Jesus Christ. I know that he became man that he might bear our sins and pity and soothe our sorrows, and I would have you know and believe in him too, for life has many burdens and many sorrows, especially for the poor and friendless, and he would fain be the God of the poor and despised—the slaves as well as free citizens."

Glaucia could not wait to hear more, but she had heard enough to make her wish for this God to be her God. If all were true that this old man said, what good news it was for the world! She had seen the altar dedicated to the "Unknown God" spoken of by the old man, and she had asked who offered sacrifice here and to which of their gods it was dedicated; but the only answer she had received was, that he had never yet left the heights of Olympus, or allowed mortal or hero to see his form. But could it be true that if he was so great he would condescend to be the God of slaves? The old man said he would, but the news seemed too great, too good, to be received very readily; and Glaucia went home in a maze of perplexing hopes and fears that made her quite forgetful of the lapse of time, and that the hour for preparing her mistress's bath had already passed.

CHAPTER IV.

LAON'S ESCAPE.

WE must return once more to the slave-market of Rome, where we left Laon. When the British slave who had carried him away from the market to the shed at the back, and laid him on the straw in the corner, saw how much he was injured, he did not think it necessary to close the door.

"He will never move again, I expect," he said softly to himself; "but he is a brave boy though a Greek, and would have made a hero if he had only been a Briton," and he turned a pitying look on the young Greek as he spoke.

Laon had not moved, or given the least sign of life; and when the slave went back he whispered to another that the boy was dead; but no one dared to mention this in the hearing of their master lest his anger should be turned against them, and it was not until after Glaucia was sold and the Briton himself had found another master that the report reached his owner's ears.

Meanwhile Laon had slowly recovered from the fainting fit, and become sensible of a burning thirst, as well as the pain and stiffness of all his limbs. How badly these were cut and bruised he did not know until he attempted to turn round to look for some water, and then, with a deep groan, fell back upon the straw. He did not attempt to move again for some minutes until the raging thirst overcame even his pain and stiffness, and by a desperate effort he at length succeeded in crawling to the door in search of water.

Not a jar or a pitcher could he see close at hand; but at some distance away, across the strip of waste ground that served for a slave-pen, he noticed a tank at which a mule was drinking, and he resolved to try and reach it, for water he must have or he would die. His anxiety concerning Glaucia, even, was swallowed up in his burning desire for a draught of water; so, painfully and with toil crawling on his hands and knees until the tank was reached, he stooped down and drank, and bathed his head and face.

To get back to the shed, however, without resting seemed an impossibility, and so he crept under a pile of loose boards close by for shelter from the blazing sun. He had not been there long before he was fast asleep. To his surprise and alarm the sun had set before he awoke, and the first sounds that met his ear were the voices of two men talking over the market business of the day.

"The Greeks are both gone," he heard him say. "Fulvius sold the girl, and kicked the boy to death!"

"Kicked him to death!" repeated the other. "He has got away, or the demons have carried off his body if he died, for no one has seen him lately."

"Poor wretch! I hope he will escape, then, for Fulvius will not give him another chance, I know. I am glad the girl is sold," he added, "and I hope she will have a good mistress."

"She was bought for one of the Gracchi; I hear it was their freedman who bought her."

Laon forgot every thing as he lay and listened with intense earnestness to these words. He was thought to be dead or to have escaped, and Glaucia was sold. His mind was soon made up how he was to act: he would make good his escape or die in the attempt, and the thought of being once more free seemed to endue him with new strength and courage, and his joy was so great that he forgot wounds and bruises, as well as the dangers by which he was surrounded.

He felt inclined to shout his rejoicings as

he lay, but prudence warned him to keep perfectly quiet for the present, and not to attempt to get further until the shadows of night had fallen. Lying there, he soon became sensible of feeling very hungry as well as thirsty; but his limbs were not so stiff as they had been in the morning, and when at last it grew dark enough for him to venture from his hiding-place he was able to walk, although with pain and difficulty.

Once away from the slave-market, he had to consider which road he should take. He was a stranger in Rome, but he thought if he could find its poorest quarter he might hide safely there for a few days, and then go in search of Glaucia, and some employment for the future. Choosing the loneliest roads, and avoiding every chance passenger he met, Laon crept on his toilsome way until he reached a narrow lane at the corner of which was a hostelry, and a group of gladiators were sitting near the threshold watching a quaternion of soldiers who, with a prisoner in charge, had just passed.

"What say you, my Lepidus, shall we see yonder Jew in the arena? Criminals have not been so plentiful of late that we can afford to let them escape when we have a fine Numidian lion to be tickled."

"How know you that the prisoner is a Jew?" asked one of his companions.

"O, 'tis easy enough to tell a Jew," said the gladiator; and he went on to talk of his supposed combatant, the "Numidian lion."

"The games must be kept up and the people amused, or they will grow dissatisfied and ask too closely about the emperor's mother and her sudden death, and why the Jewish proselyte, Poppæa, sits on the throne of Octavia."

"Our Nero would know how to answer them, as well as how to play on the lute before them," replied another carelessly.

"Thou art a mole, Burbo, and, by the helmet of Cesar, thou wilt never be any wiser. Didst thou not hear to-day that Poppæa hated this Jew as much as those who brought him from Judea? Now canst thou not see why he will be condemned?"

"To please Poppæa thou wouldst say," replied the other sullenly.

"To please Poppæa and Rome too. All men hate this new sect called Christians, of which this prisoner is the champion; but to see him in the arena with the lion will please them better than seeing Nero himself. Indeed, I have heard it whispered that they have wearied somewhat of our emperor's performances of late."

"'Tis well they never weary of the sword and cestus, or what would become of our trade?" And the speaker stretched out his brawny arms as he spoke, and almost knocked Laon down, who had paused to rest rather too near the group.

"By Pollux, there is some one here!" he said, jumping up as he spoke, and the next minute Laon found himself in the vice-like grip of the brawny gladiator, who dragged him out of the shadow into the full glare of the light. "Now, then, who art thou that comest creeping in the way of a gladiator?" continued the man, giving him a shake that almost threw him down.

Laon was trembling with apprehension, but he looked up boldly in the man's face as he answered, "I am a Greek, and a stranger in Rome."

"Greek or Roman, by the helmet of Cesar, thou wouldst make a fine gladiator," said the man, looking at the boy's limbs admiringly.

"He looks as though he had been in the arena already," said another, noticing the wounds and bruises on his face, arms, and legs.

Laon was in an agony of terror lest his secret should be discovered, or they should suspect he was a runaway slave; so he said quickly, "Do gladiators earn money?"

A loud burst of laughter greeted this question. " Dost thou think we train ourselves into beasts for the love of it ? " asked one.

" We come to love it at last, though," put in another.

"Ah, when a gladiator has once seen blood he is like the tiger that tastes it, he is ever craving for more and more ! 'Tis a glorious life, and a merry one, I can tell thee, boy. Hast thou a mind to be a gladiator ? " he asked.

" I want to earn some money as soon as I can," said Laon dubiously.

" And thou thinkest it can be done in the arena. Well, thou talkest like a brave lad, though I doubt not thou hast run away from home, and thy mother is crying her eyes out for thee ; and thou yet bearest the marks of thy father's whipping."

" I have neither father nor mother," said Laon, " but I have a sister I want to help."

" Gladiators are best without sisters. 'Tis the thought of the weak women-kind that is apt to make cowards of them when they should be brave, and face death with a shout as loud as the audience and the emperor himself."

" I should not like to die until I have saved Glaucia," murmured Laon, half to himself and half aloud.

"There is no favor shown in the arena, and thy blood is as likely to soak the spoliarium when thou art dragged out as that thou shouldst tap a fresh wine skin with the sestertia thou hast earned. What sayest thou, boy, canst thou brave the chances and enter the lists with us? Our master is in want of a few more pupils, and I'll promise thee entrance at our school, and no questions asked, either."

This last promise had more weight with Laon than any thing else, and he boldly answered, "We can but die once, and I may live to see Glaucia free."

"Well done, youngster! Said I not he was a brave fellow?" added the man, turning to his companions. "Pass down the drinking-cups," he commanded; "he shall taste of the wine that fires a true gladiator's blood;" and the cup was placed in Laon's hand.

He sipped a little, but, truth to tell, he would greatly have preferred a draught of cold water and a few green figs to the choicest wine in Rome; but he was afraid to tell his rough hosts, and so he tried to drink as much of their sour wine as he could.

"So thou art a stranger in Rome?" said the one who had put most of the questions to him, and appeared to be the leader of the party.

"Yes, I came from Athens but a few weeks since."

"And thought to find the imperial city paved with gold, I'll warrant," said the man.

"I had rather it were strewn with green figs just now," replied Laon; "but neither figs nor gold seem very plentiful here."

"Wait till thou winnest the purse of gold in the arena," said one. "Thou wilt have something better than green figs."

"But if I wait until then I shall not want them at all," said Laon. Hunger was making him bold; but his boldness pleased the men much better than any thing else could have done; and one of them called to the landlord to bring some green figs and bread at once, and Laon was ordered to eat as much as he could.

"Eat like a gladiator, though it is not gladiators' food," said one as he pushed the supper toward the boy.

Laon needed no second bidding, for he had not tasted food since the morning, and as he ate he listened eagerly to the talk going on around him, for it had turned upon the great families of Rome who patronized and encouraged the games. He hoped to hear that of the Gracchi—he had not forgotten the name mentioned by the man when talking of Glaucia—

and he resolved to ask some questions about them—where they lived, and whether they were reputed to be kind to their slaves.

But, to his disappointment, although several patrician families were talked about, this was not one of them. These men, rough and coarse as they were, gave instruction, it seemed, to some of the proudest families of Rome in the use of boxing-gloves and short stick, and these were talked of quite freely, but no one mentioned the name he was longing to hear.

When the men had finished their carousal, and rose to go home, one of them asked the landlord of the inn to let Laon sleep under the benches, promising to call for him in the morning to take him to the school and introduce him to the master.

The landlord looked suspiciously at Laon, but did not like to offend his rough customers by a refusal, especially when he heard that Laon himself was to be trained for a gladiator, and so bade him welcome to a heap of straw that lay in the back part of the house, which was certainly better accommodation than Laon had expected to receive.

Early the next morning he was awakened by the low growl of a dog, and springing to his feet as quickly as his stiffened limbs would allow, he saw the surly-looking landlord gazing earnestly at him.

"Well, my young bacchanalian, thou mayest feast at the gladiator's expense, but thou shalt not at mine, for if thou art not a runaway slave I never saw one."

Laon turned crimson, but did not lose his presence of mind. "I am a Greek," he said quickly, "and how call ye one of my nation a slave?"

"Ye are all slaves," said the man sneeringly; "thy country is but a Roman province, subject to the laws and will of the emperor, like all the rest of the world."

Laon clenched his fist angrily. "Are there no heroes but Romans, think ye?" he asked; then, remembering that if it came to an open quarrel between them he should inevitably get worsted and perhaps lose his freedom again, he wisely turned away without saying any more, and went out into the lane to watch for his friend the gladiator.

The place was busy enough now in the early morning sunshine, for the country people living in the villages outside the city walls were bringing in fruit and vegetables, ice and flowers, and were urging on their pannier-laden mules with shouts and blows quite as lustily bestowed as by any modern street-seller of the present day. Laon had to keep very close to the threshold, and occasionally dive inside a house, to avoid being run over, for the street was narrow and the traffic considerable; and there being no pathway for the convenience of foot-passengers, they had to thread their way between the vehicles, or dive and dodge along from doorway to doorway in a fashion more exciting than agreeable. Some of the streets of his native Athens were no better, so that the sight was not altogether new to Laon; and yet he stood idly watching one after another as they passed him and went up the street, until he felt positively interested in their various movements.

At last his attention was caught by a young girl, who came carefully picking her way along by the wall, listening, as it seemed, rather than looking, at the vehicles as they passed. Moving a little closer, Laon saw that her eyes were closed, and at the same time a man called out to a clumsy market woman, who was urging her mule close to the wall, "Mind the blind girl!"

Whether she heard or not, she paid no heed to the caution, and Laon darted out and dragged the girl inside the door only in time to prevent her being run over.

"I give thee thanks," said the girl, gently lifting her sightless but now widely-opened eyes to Laon's face. They were lovely eyes, dark and liquid in spite of their blindness.

"Thou shouldst not come out alone," said Laon as he watched for an opportunity to place her in the right direction.

"I am quite used to going about the city by myself, but this morning errand is the worst I have to perform," she said, and then, for the first time, Laon noticed that she carried a small basket in her hand.

"Let me carry this and guide thee as far as thou art going," said Laon, attempting to take the basket from her as he spoke.

But the girl would not give it up.

"No, no," she said, "it is not heavy, I can carry it myself; but if thou art not busy and can go with me to the end of the lane, I shall feel thankful."

"I will go with thee until thou art out of danger," said Laon, and he took the girl's hand as he spoke, and she once more stepped out into the bustling crowd.

They walked on to the end of the lane, Laon carefully guarding and guiding his companion all the way. She wanted him to leave her then, but he refused to do so, for the street they were now in was wider but quite as crowded, and so this was passed, and then another, and they began to draw near the military quarter of the city. At one of the houses a soldier was posted, plainly showing that a prisoner lodged there, and before this the blind girl stopped.

"I am grateful for thy kindness to one so helpless and friendless," she said, turning toward him before she ascended the steps; "I cannot reward thee, but the Lord will at the day of his appearing," she added, and she was allowed to enter the house without a word of question from the sentinel on duty.

CHAPTER V.

THE MYSTERIOUS PRISONER

LAON stood looking at the house after the girl had entered it, wondering who the prisoner within could be, and half disposed to wait until she came out again to question her. To speak to the sentinel standing in front was useless; he might as well question the statue of Apollo opposite, for the result would be the same; and so, after a few minutes, he wandered back to the hostelry just in time to meet the gladiator, who had come to take him to the school.

"Hast thou had any thing to eat, boy?" he asked, clapping him on the shoulder with rough good humor.

"No; I have been through the streets but found neither gold nor green figs," said Laon, smiling.

"Green figs!" repeated the gladiator contemptuously, and he struck his giant-like fist on one of the stands near, and called, in a stentorian voice, "Serve us some meat quick, or, by Jupiter, I will kill and eat thee!"

The landlord was used to his customer, and came forward with a dish of half-raw meat, smiling as pleasantly as possible.

"There, boy, that's worth all the green figs in the market," said the gladiator, seizing a piece and pushing the rest toward Laon.

He looked as though he would dispute this statement. Figs would have been much more to his taste than such meat as this, but he was hungry, and, moreover, very unwilling to offend his benefactor; but he could not wholly repress his disgust as he looked at the half-raw, coarse food, and the man noticed it.

"Come, youngster, thou wilt never make one of our brave band if thou disdainest our food," he said, in a half-offended tone.

"I am not used to it," said Laon; and after he had eaten a few mouthfuls he pushed the dish aside. "Thanks for my first gladiator meal," he said; "I am now ready for the work."

"Thou'lt never be fit for our work unless thou dost eat our food," said the man; "but thou shalt see some of it this morning. Come along," he added, striding out as he spoke.

The renowned school of the gladiators was not far off, and in a few minutes Laon was introduced to the master of the establishment. He looked critically at the new comer, felt his joints, grunted at the cuts and bruises about his arms and legs, and then told him he might stand aside and see the exercises of the men, who were standing about in groups, while along the walls hung tridents, nets, swords, and the various weapons used in the arena.

The master, who was himself a retired gladiator, treated his big, powerful pupils as though they were veritable school-boys. Commanding silence as he advanced to the middle of the room, he ordered one to take down the various appliances ready for use, stamping, swearing, and threatening when one was touched unscientifically or carelessly. Then two were ordered to engage in apparently mortal combat, the rest standing round watching and listening to the directions of the master, who kept his eye on every movement of the men, and shouted his commands to close, to parry, to thrust, first to one and then to the other, their companions commenting meanwhile on every vigorous move or every false thrust, which the combatants knew would be brought against them afterward.*

Laon stood and watched these exercises with great interest at first, but still he felt no wish to join in them, no desire to buckle on the

* See Frontispiece.

cestus or throw the net, and he began to weary of the whole before they were over. His thoughts had wandered off to the blind girl and the words she had uttered when leaving him: "I cannot reward thee, but the Lord will at the day of his appearing."

Laon remembered the words and repeated them several times to himself. "I do not want any reward," he said, "but I would like to know who she means by 'the Lord.' Is she the slave of some great Roman who has a special favor toward her, and is expected to return by and by, or is it her master that is a prisoner now, I wonder?"

Thinking of this, Laon quite forgot where he was until the exercises for the day came to an end, when, without further notice of him, the master walked away, and the gladiators, like school-boys, began hectoring each other, or betting on the skill with which they would kill each other the next time they appeared in the arena. To hear them, one would think they were of less value than the beasts of the field, and hated each other like furies. And yet they were good friends enough, only that every feeling common to humanity, and which makes man better than the brutes, had been debased, trampled upon, and almost trodden out of these men, until they were more brutish than the beasts with whom they often fought.

Something of this feeling stole into Laon's heart as he followed his friend out into the street. "I shall never be a gladiator because I like it," he said softly to himself, "but I will learn to use the cestus and trident for the sake of Glaucia."

"Well, my young friend, what is that thou art saying?" asked the gladiator suddenly.

Laon colored. "For my sister's sake I should like to learn how to use the trident and net, as well as the cestus," replied Laon.

The man shook his head. "The net and trident are the most dangerous weapons," he said.

"Come, come, Appius, thou art wasting our time, and, by Venus, that is not needful when so many bright eyes are waiting for us in the proudest halls of Rome," said one of his companions, frowning at Laon as he spoke.

Appius saw the frown. "I have taken the boy under my protection," he said, "and he shall come with us to drink of our next wine-skin; and if I should, by and by, give him a mortal thrust and send him to the fields of Elysium, he will forgive me, and know it was done in fair fight."

"No one accuses thee of fighting unfairly,

Appius, any more than they believe in thy Elysium, or the fable invented by the philosophers, that death is not the end of us."

"You believe as—"

"I believe in the gods, so let us hasten to pour a libation to Bacchus," interrupted another; and, motioning Laon to keep close beside him, Appius led the way to the hostelry, where, by the appearance of the wine-cups and half-cooked meats, they were evidently expected.

Appius, as the leader of the party, took his seat first, and, taking up a wine-cup, bowed reverentially to the statue opposite, saying as he did so, "Be propitious, O Bacchus!" and then, sprinkling a little of the wine on the table, the meal began.

Appius considerately ordered a dish of green figs to be brought for Laon, and when the meal was over, and they were dispersing until the evening, he told him he might come to share their meal then, and he would take him to the school again in the morning.

Laon scarcely knew what to do with himself for the remaining hours of the day. He felt half afraid of going about the streets for fear of being seen and recognized by his late master or some of his fellow-slaves, and yet he was anxious to discover where Glaucia was living.

The point as to whether he should go out or stay indoors was settled for him by the landlord of the hostelry, who, seeing him still lingering near the door after the gladiators had left, threatened to kick him out if he did not go at once. So Laon wandered up the lane, mechanically taking the same road he had traversed with the blind girl in the morning, until at length he again found himself standing before the house with its sentinel in front. But for this he might have failed to recognize it, for it was not by any means distinguishable either by its luxury or poverty, but a small, plain, middle-class residence, such as respectable people might inhabit but the wealthy would disdain.

Laon had a peep at its interior as he stood loitering outside, and he noticed that the vestibule was quite plain, and the atrium beyond was entirely without ornament—at least so far as he could see from his post of observation; and his surprise was increased when he saw a litter stop close to the steps, and an elegantly dressed lady, attended by a female slave, walk in.

"It must be a great man imprisoned here," said Laon softly to himself; "I wonder what his crime can be."

In a few minutes two other people came up

the street and stole into the house, but they did not appear to be wealthy, and yet somewhat above the dependent condition of freedmen. As Laon stood there watching, a dozen people at least went in unquestioned, unchallenged by the sentry, who nevertheless, he could see, looked at each. Had these been people of one rank in life this fact would not have been so noticeable; but the first lady was evidently a foreigner, and the dress of her lictors, still waiting about, proclaimed them to be of Cesar's household. Then, there were merchants from his own country; two or three stately-looking Jews; some working people, both men and women, and slaves of both sexes.

What a strange company for one such house to contain at the same time! Were they all going to visit the same person? would they all meet in that undecorated atrium? Laon wished he could get another glimpse of it; but the curtain had been dropped between that and the vestibule, and its heavy folds shut out all inquisitive glances, so, at last, he went away, feeling very curious as to this mysterious house and its strange occupant. But, before leaving, he looked closely at the litter, with its silken curtains embroidered with silver and bearing the imperial arms of Nero. Could the lady he had seen be the Jewish proselyte, Poppæa, whom the gladiators were talking of both last night and this morning? She was said to favor the Jews, and they enjoyed more freedom just now in consequence of it. Perhaps this prisoner was a Jew: and then he suddenly remembered the blind girl, and that she would know all about it, and so he resolved to ask her the downright question, "Did she go to visit the Jewish prisoner?" the very next time he saw her.

He wandered on up the street and down the lane, past the hostelry, in hope of seeing her, but she did not come in his way; and every effort he made to discover the whereabouts of Glaucia was equally unsuccessful.

He had his supper and spent the night at the hostelry again, and the next morning had the pleasure of seeing the blind girl come carefully feeling her way as before. He went to meet her at once, saying gently, "I will lead thee past these mules and carts;" and he led her up the lane.

When they got to the more quiet neighborhood, Laon put the question, which he thought would startle and surprise, perhaps very much alarm, her; but he spoke in an undertone, that no one else might hear the whispered words, "Art thou going to the Jewish prisoner again?"

But, to his surprise, she answered quite calmly, "Yes, my mistress sends his morning meal by my hands;" and then she asked, "Hast thou been to see him?"

"Been to see him—who? the Lord thou spake of the other day?" said Laon.

"No; Paul, our great teacher, is not the Lord, but his servant," said the blind girl; "he would welcome thee as he does all who desire to learn this great truth that hath so lately been made known to the world."

"What truth?" anxiously asked Laon. "Tell me."

"That God is love, and sent his Son to reveal it, and die to redeem us from the power of sin and all evil," said the girl reverently.

"Then this prisoner is a messenger sent from Olympus, the dwelling of the gods," said Laon. "It is passing strange that he should not first have delivered it at Athens," he uttered incredulously.

"Nay, but our teacher cometh not from Thessaly, but from Tarsus, and is a Jew, as thou sayest, howbeit he hath been to Athens I have heard."

"Then he cometh with a message from the God of the Jews!"

"Yes, he bringeth a message from our God,

but it is to all people, not us Jews only," said the girl.

"And thou art a Jewess," uttered Laon in a tone of surprise.

"I am," replied the blind girl, and she said it quite as proudly as a Roman dame would declare her nationality.

Laon looked puzzled. "Thou sayest this teacher is a Jew, and bringest a message to all people; but each nation hath its own gods."

"They are false gods, the work of men's hands; wood and stone, that can neither feel nor understand."

Laon looked hurt and surprised. "Hush! hush!" he said, "we know they are the work of men's hands, but they are men whom the gods have inspired to make a dwelling-place meet for them to inhabit—a dwelling-place that shall teach us the special care or delight of the indwelling God."

But the Jewess shook her head. "There is but one God," she said, "and the idols he will utterly abolish."

Laon looked offended. "What!" he exclaimed, "doth thy God claim to be greater than our Pallas Athene, or Jupiter himself?"

"These are but idols," said the blind girl.

"And this man hath come to declare that the

gods of Athens and Rome are but idols, and that only the Jews' God is worthy the name!" said Laon angrily. "I do not wonder he is a prisoner," he went on. "Could any thing be more insulting to us, to our heroes and philosophers? Would this new teacher set himself above the wise men of our Greece, who are learned in all the wisdom of the world, and of the gods too; who understand magic, and charms, and all knowledge pertaining to the sun, moon, and stars?"

"They are but heathen, blind and ignorant, worshiping they know not what," said the girl, almost as warmly as Laon himself had been speaking.

"Blind and ignorant," repeated Laon passionately. "Thou callest our Plato and Socrates blind and ignorant, and wouldst have me believe in this new teacher of thy unknown God."

"Yes, I would have thee come and hear for thyself this truth, that gives freedom to the world; that makes all men equal in the sight of God, whether Jew or Gentile, slave or freeborn."

"I will not come," said Laon decisively. "Do you think I would listen while this vain, arrogant man set himself up above our heroes and philosophers, and even the gods themselves? By the helmet of Cesar, he should be thrown to the wild beasts in the arena if I were the emperor," he added energetically.

"I am sorry it should make thee angry," said the blind girl after a lengthened pause. "I had hoped thou wouldst have come sometimes to listen to the gracious words that fall from our great teacher's lips."

Laon shook his head. "What is this man's name?" he asked.

"He is called Brother Paul now, but in former days he was called Saul."

"I shall not forget the name," said Laon, as he turned away. He could not help feeling disappointed at the abrupt termination of this new friendship; but the girl had insulted the gods, and how could he be friends with one who spoke slightingly of Pallas Athene?

CHAPTER VI.

THE FEAST OF BACCHUS.

LAON wandered on after leaving the blind girl, quite forgetful of the danger he incurred of being seen by his former master, thinking by turns of what he had just heard and of his sister, wondering where she was.

"I will find out to-day," he said at length. "I will search all over Rome until I find this family who have bought her," and he set off at once on his quest, taking no heed of the splendid chariots or elegantly dressed occupants any more than he did of the foot passengers or the public notices posted on the walls giving information of when the games would take place, and what the spectacle would be, the feasts of the different gods to be observed, as well as the edicts of the emperor.

Had Laon only paused to listen to the talk going on around him, or noticed the eager rush all the fashionable part of Rome was making in one direction, he would have found that the feast of Bacchus was to be observed that day, and that he was hastening to the place appointed as well as the rest. Had he known it he would certainly have gone in an opposite direction, for he was in no mood for feasting and reveling just now, and then he was more likely to meet some who knew him at such a place of public resort ; but his first intimation of this fact came when it was too late for him to turn back.

The procession itself was near, but in advance of all the rest walked, or rather skipped and danced, a young Bacchante, her head and shoulders wreathed with vine leaves, and madly intoxicated, or pretending to be so, in honor of the god of which she was the priestess. In a moment she had caught him in her arms, and went on whirling and dancing with him, while merry shouts and laughter greeted them on every side, and the music of the procession seemed to urge her on to greater wildness in her processional dance.

Laon tried to get away once or twice, but finding this was impossible, he joined in the fun, like the rest, though now and then the thought of what the blind girl had said that morning came back to his mind ; but there was less horror in it now in the midst of all this revelry, for it was impossible for the Jews' God to be worse than their Bacchus, and if he were better, would it not be well to allow him a place in their Pantheon, that the worship prescribed for him might correct some of the evils connected with these infamous feasts?

How infamous and abominable they were Laon never knew until he was dragged into participating in them, and his whole soul sickened and revolted at the drunkenness and vile obscenity of the whole. The thought of Glaucia ever seeing or hearing what he had that day witnessed made him shudder; and yet it seemed that people grew so accustomed to such scenes that they could enjoy them, at least, for there was no lack of visitors, and they by no means the lowest of Roman society.

What time the revel was at length over Laon never knew, but he managed to get away soon after the shadows of evening had deepened into night; early enough for him to pass through the streets without exciting attention, but too late to get back to the hostelry where he had promised to meet his friend, the gladiator. So he crept into a half-ruinous house that he saw near at hand, resolving to go to the training school early the next day.

He awoke at daylight the next morning, and after a draught of water from a neighboring fountain, set off on his way back to the part of the city with which he was most familiar, and again found himself before the mysterious house which had already given rise in various ways to so many perplexing thoughts. Again a litter stopped in front, and a lady stepped from it; but instead of hastening up the steps, she stopped and looked searchingly at Loan.

"Art thou one to be trusted?" she asked.

The boy looked his surprise at the strange question. "The only proof I can give is, in the performance of the service required, for I am a stranger in Rome," he said.

"Then I am afraid thou wilt not be able to do what I wish," she said, glancing at the waxen tablets she held in her hand and then at the slaves who had borne her litter. "No, I cannot spare either of them to go," she said aloud, as if answering a mental question, "and yet if they have not yet left Rome, as I hear they have not, I should like my Romola to receive this letter of thanks, for it was kind, very kind, to make me the offer she did."

She seemed to forget the presence of Laon as she said this softly to herself, and he stood silently wondering whether this lady was about to visit this strange, vain prisoner, who claimed so much honor for his God. At length she said,

"I think I can make thee understand how to find Romola Gracchi, for their house is just beyond the Porta Capena," she said, delivering the tablets, carefully bound together with scarlet silk, into his hands as she spoke.

Laon started at the mention of the name, and now looked up eagerly into her face. "Yes, I shall be sure to find it," he said quickly; "I would search Rome all over to—to—" and then he stammered and blushed.

But the lady did not notice his confusion. "Thou hast but to ask for the Porta Capena," she said, "and just beyond the walls is the villa of 'Plane Trees,' any little goat-herd thou mayest meet can tell thee where it is, and ask to see the noble Romola Gracchi, and deliver this letter into her hands, but to no other. Should the slaves ask to take it from thee, tell them thou art the bearer of a message from Julia to their mistress, for I would fain know whether they have in truth left the city, or are detained, as my slave informed me."

Laon took the delicate white tablets, and, clasping them tightly in his hands, walked quickly away in the direction of the southern gate. The lady may have been a little surprised at the eagerness of her messenger, but she would have been more so had she followed him a short distance, for along the next street there stood a statue of Minerva, and when the boy reached it he stopped, and, bowing reverently, said aloud, "Be propitious, O Pallas Athene, and lead my steps to Glaucia once more."

He then hurried on past the Forum, and by the same route his sister had gone a day or two before, until he passed through the Porta Capena, and then he began to inquire for the villa of "Plane Trees." He had little difficulty in finding it, but he heard, to his disappointment, that it was empty before he reached it.

"The family are gone to Athens, and not likely to return for some years," said an old slave who lived in the neighborhood, and who seemed to know the whole of its affairs.

He noticed the look of disappointment that overspread Laon's face as he heard this.

"Wert thou particularly interested in finding them?" he said, glancing at the letter in his hand.

"Yes," answered Laon, "my sister lived with them, I hear." He could not bring himself to say "sold" to them.

"Was she a fair-haired slave, bought for the imperious Valeria the day before they left?"

"I know not for whom she was bought, but

she was sold three days since, and I am anxious to find her," answered Laon.

The old man nodded, and said, "It is the same, I doubt not; and she must beware not to displease her mistress Valeria, or—" and he pointed significantly toward a piece of ground opposite.

"What do you mean?" asked Laon.

"What! your sister a slave in Rome, and you don't know *that?*" said the man.

Laon shook his head. "What is it?" he asked.

"Come and see," said the old man in a mysterious whisper, leading the way as he spoke.

Laon followed, looking intently in the direction indicated, but it was not until a turn in the road was reached that he could see any thing; but then it burst upon his view all at once, the sickening, agonizing view of five crosses planted in the earth, and a dead, dying, or writhing victim upon each. The boy covered his face with his hands and uttered a scream of horror. He could not ask what crimes these men had committed, but a group of travelers, who were evidently on their way to Rome, asked this question in a foreign accent.

To them the old man bowed, and replied, "They are slaves."

"But their crime?" demanded one of the foreigners.

The old man shook his head. "They may be guilty of crime, or they may have offended their master—who can tell? 'Tis easy to get a slave condemned to the cross."

"And this is the boasted Roman civilization!" said another angrily; "truly this Rome is more admirable in the distance than on a close view. None can fail to admire her great works—her roads and bridges, by which mountains are leveled, valleys filled up, and the rivers made fordable at all times; and we thought the gods must dwell with such a people, and we have come from the land beyond the mountains to see whether Rome is another name for Asgard."

"The gods dwell not at Rome, but on Mount Olympus, in our Greece," said Laon quickly.

"Are the Greeks greater than the Romans, then? Do ye make better roads? Have ye framed better laws? Are ye—"

"Greece is but a Roman province now," interrupted the old slave. "I know nothing about its roads or its laws, but I know it had to bow to the arms of Rome, like every other nation," he added.

"And this—this is part of thy civilization!"

said the stranger, glancing once more at the sickening spectacle close at hand.

No one replied to this, and, with a puzzled look, the strangers passed on, and Laon was left with the old slave.

"They would not treat a woman—a girl—in this way!" he said, turning away that he might not see the hideous crosses.

"No one knows what they will do next," said his companion. "Rome is rotten, boy—rotten at its core! The Romans of to-day are not heroes—scarcely men; the worship of the old gods is decaying, and every body is looking out for a new god and a new religion. The worship of the Egyptian Isis is the fashion now, but who can say that the miserable sect called Nazarenes may not be in the ascendant next moon."

"Who are they?" asked Laon as he walked back toward the gate of the city.

"Well, I have heard they are a sect of the Jews, or at least the Jews' God is worshiped, and that one pretending to be his messenger is even now in prison here."

"Is he called Paul?" asked Laon quickly.

"Nay, I know not; but I would fain be glad to find him, for there is a rumor that this religion is for slaves, and I have not heard of such as that before."

"I have seen slaves go to the house where this same Paul is imprisoned," said Laon, "and likewise merchants and great ladies."

"Yes, all classes are tainted with this restless desire to find a new god, but what he is to be when our whole Pantheon will not satisfy us, I cannot tell. But you said you knew where this same Paul was to be found. I have an hour to spare now, will you guide me to him? for I would fain ask him a few questions about his God."

Laon made no objection to the man's accompanying him back; indeed, he was rather glad of the opportunity it gave him of asking some questions about the family of the Gracchi. The account he received was not very encouraging, for, judging by the various tales told by the old man, they were a proud, stern, haughty family, whom few could please and none satisfy.

The boy heaved a deep sigh. "I must go to Athens and find Glaucia," he whispered softly to himself, and then, for the first time, he recollected that, not being able to deliver the letter with which he had been intrusted, he ought to return it to the lady, but that he did not know her name or where she lived, and had not even seen her face, as she was closely vailed.

At last he said, "If thou dost go into the house to speak to this prisoner, Paul, I will go with thee."

"Very well; I am a slave, and thy sister is a slave, and so if there is good news for me there will be for her," said the old man.

"And for me, too," said Laon; and then, suddenly recollecting that he ought not to betray the secret of his escape to a stranger, he added, "I love Glaucia as my own life."

Laon had half expected to see the litter still waiting outside the door where he had left it, but it was not there, and so he ventured to cross the threshold after muttering a few mys tical words that were to break the spell of any evil that the strange prisoner might otherwise work upon him.

It was with a half-frightened, half-defiant feeling that Laon passed through the vestibule and entered the atrium where Paul, the aged prisoner, sat, chained by the wrist and ankle to a rough-looking soldier, who nevertheless relaxed so far as to smile a welcome to the boy when he saw him inclined to run away again.

"Be not afraid, my son," said the prisoner himself in a voice of tenderness and yet of command.

Lifting his eyes to the venerable face, he saw

that it was pale, thin, and wrinkled, but with such a look of sweet majesty upon it that Laon instinctively bowed his head in reverence, while his heart went forth in love toward the man who had been such a puzzle to him. *He* was worthy to be the messenger of any of the gods, he thought; and then his thoughts went back to the feast of Bacchus, and he recalled the besotted, brutalized faces of the wine-god priests, and compared them with the calm, spiritual grandeur of this man's, who welcomed the old slave and himself with as much polite courtesy as though they were the highest patricians of Rome.

He was surprised at the size of the atrium, and the accommodation it afforded for a large number of people to assemble in it. He judged that the peristyle and viridarium had been thrown into this one large hall. His companion was evidently as much surprised as himself at all he saw, but he ventured to put the questions he had come to ask, and which were kindly and graciously answered.

"I come as the messenger of God to all men, whether bond or free; and my message, that Christ Jesus came into the world to make known the love of God to all men, and then died to redeem them, is worthy the acceptation of all."

"But this is the Jews' God," objected the old slave.

"He is the God of the Gentile as well as the Jew, the only true almighty, eternal, ever-present God, the great ONE not to be equaled or approached by any thing calling itself god in heaven above or in the earth beneath."

"But our Jupiter and Mars, surely they are gods," said the old slave.

The benign countenance looked pitingly at the old man's evident pain and perplexity. "Men have walked in darkness, serving vain idols instead of the true God, but the light has come at last," said Paul.

"And it needs must dazzle the eyes at first, I judge," said the old slave. "I will come again if I can, but I cannot hear more now," and he departed, leaving Laon to ask about the letter he still held in his hand—how he should return it to the lady who gave it to him.

"I will take charge of it and deliver it when she comes again," said the prisoner; and with a parting blessing he dismissed Laon, thinking he wished to join his companion.

CHAPTER VII.

AT SEA.

LAON left the prison-house with a strange feeling of mingled surprise and regret—regret that he had not been to see this strange messenger from the gods before; regret, too, that he had seen him at all, for he must try and find his way to Athens in search of Glaucia, so that he was not likely to see him or hear any thing of his message again, and this visit had made him more than ever dissatisfied with the priests of all the favorite deities. He hastened to overtake the old slave who had accompanied him, and ask his opinion about what he had heard. But the old man did not seem willing to talk about it.

"I must go again, my son, and hear more of this strange doctrine," he said. "If our supposed light has been darkness, then the true light will dazzle at first. But is it the true light? Is this message from the Regenerator—the Freedom-giver the world has been looking for so eagerly of late?"

"Has the world been looking for such a messenger?" asked Laon.

"Has it? Ah, boy, you are young and I am a slave, but I can interpret this rushing after every new god which possesses our people. Some are throwing themselves at the feet of this Egyptian Isis; while others, like Fabrizzio Gracchi, are seeking in the study of philosophy the answer to this questioning and longing. But what if it should come, after all, to slaves first, in words that they and every man and woman can understand, instead of through the wisdom and learning of the great and wise! This alone would dazzle, boy, and I would think over in quiet what I have heard to-day."

But Laon wanted to find out all he could concerning the family who had taken Glaucia away, and so he still kept by the old man's side. "Thou spakest of Fabrizzio Gracchi and his love of philosophy; hath he gone to Athens to study in our Academy?" he said.

The old man nodded. "Fabrizzio is one of the few Romans left who will not bow down and worship Cæsar. Patriotism hath ever been the god and the worship of the Gracchi, and patriotism is dead in Rome now—dead and buried; and so the heart of the proud Gracchi is hungering, like many another here, for something higher and purer than the blind bowing down before the emperor."

Laon thought that the poor old man, being dissatisfied with his own condition, supposed every body else must be the same, so he said, rather abruptly, "Can you tell me the way to Athens?"

If he had asked the way to the moon the old man could not have looked more surprised. "The way to Athens, boy!" he said, "how will you get there?"

Laon, who knew nothing of geography, and supposed the world to be one vast plane, answered quickly, "I will walk there."

"Did you walk when you came here?" asked the slave.

"No, we came in a galley; but I have no money to pay the master to take me back that way, and so I must walk," said Laon.

"That is impossible. I have heard you can only go by sea to the far-off Greece," said the old man in a compassionate tone.

A look of blank despair had come into Laon's face as he heard these words. Was he never to see Glaucia again—never to have the opportunity of whispering a word of warning to her about the fate that might await her if she offended her imperious mistress? "O Pallas

Athene, art thou so angry that thou wilt not help me now!" he exclaimed.

The old man shook his head. "I have prayed to Jupiter and all the gods in turn to help me in my misery, but no answer ever came. The happy, careless, smiling gods cannot be troubled with the tears of mortals; they only accept our garlands and sacrifices, and smile on our feasts —our woes do not trouble them."

"Because we are slaves, you would say," answered Laon bitterly; "then I will search for the God who hears slaves." And without another word he walked on, scarce knowing which road he took, until he found himself close to the school of the gladiators, when it suddenly occurred to him that he might ask his friend Appius to tell him how he might earn a few sesterces to pay his passage to Athens.

The slave at the door recognized him again, so he had no difficulty in gaining an entrance, and after watching the various exercises he followed the gladiators into the street, and then, gently touching the arm of his friend, asked if he could speak to him.

"What, my young pupil returned! They said thou hadst gone off with a Bacchante, and had left Rome," exclaimed the man.

"I do want to leave Rome," said Laon; "I

want to go back to my Athens. Wilt thou tell me how I can earn a few sesterces to pay the shipmaster to take me?"

The gladiators laughed. "A very fine tale!" two or three exclaimed. "Thou wast at the feast of Bacchus yesterday; where is the Bachchante that placed her garlands around thy head?"

Laon blushed as he recalled this scene. "I know not," he answered.

"But thou art anxious to discover her again, and so would fain consult the Delphic oracle!" exclaimed one.

"Nay, it is my sister I am anxious to find," said Laon quickly.

"I told these gladiators they must have no sisters, and thou art to be one now, boy," said Appius.

"Nay, but I will not, unless it is to save Glaucia," said Laon.

"Say you so, boy! Then come not near me again," said Appius, frowning darkly, and as he spoke he pushed Laon so violently that he fell to the ground, while the rest laughed at his fall as they passed on toward the hostelry for their evening meal.

Laon was not hurt much, and soon rose to his feet, but he did not follow the gladiators.

He had learned the way to the landing-places on the banks of the Tiber, and he went in that direction now, although his hopes and intentions were as yet of the vaguest. He had a few sesterces which the lady had put into his hand when she gave him the letter, and he resolved to offer these to the first shipmaster he could find going to Athens, in the hope that he would take them, and let him make up the deficiency by assisting the sailors at their work.

The docks were reached at last, and Laon, volunteering to assist in unloading a vessel, was soon set to work, and from his companions he heard that the galley had just arrived from Athens with a cargo of corn and honey, and would return thither in a few days. His heart beat high with hope as he heard it. If he could only take the place of one of the sailors—and he heard that one had already left the vessel—he might reach his native city without any further difficulty.

No one had any reason to complain of the way he performed his work that day, and when he was leaving at night he was told to come again in the morning, a command he very readily obeyed. In the course of the day he contrived to speak to the shipmaster about being taken as a sailor for the next voyage.

The man looked doubtful, but promised to consider his request, and asked him some questions about his friends, and how long since he had left Athens.

Fortunately Laon was able to answer without betraying his secret—not that he would have hesitated to tell a falsehood had it been necessary. He knew nothing of the *sin* of lying—the gods whom he looked up to with reverential awe were themselves liars, thieves, and murderers, according to the popular legends concerning them. The shipmaster seemed satisfied with the account Laon gave of himself, and seeing he was able and willing to be useful, engaged him the next day to go with him to Athens.

"We shall see then whether thou art fit for a sailor," said the man; "and if not, thou canst go to thy friends."

How grateful Laon felt to the man, and how slowly the remaining days seemed to pass, haunted as he was by that awful scene he had witnessed outside the gate of the city, and thinking it possible that his beloved sister might be doomed to a similar fate if she failed to please her mistress. If he could only see her he might warn her to be careful, and encourage her to be patient, as he would speedily release her from her present state of bondage.

The weary days, long as they were, came to an end at last, and Laon was floating down the muddy Tiber toward the blue sea that was to bear him to the city of temples, the dwelling-place of the gods, the "Eye of Greece." The lad's heart beat high with hope. He would redeem his sister from slavery or die in the attempt. He would go and see some of their old friends among the citizens and ask them to help him to do this, if he could not accomplish it alone.

"Be propitious, O Venus!" he exclaimed. "If Pallas Athene be vengeful and angry, be thou the more favorable!"

"Who is it that thou art beseeching, boy?" asked one of the sailors, who happened to be standing near. "The Dioscuri—the twin stars, these be the guardian god of sailors. Didst thou ever sacrifice to them?"

Laon was obliged to confess he had never heard of this deity before. "I thought Venus, who rose from the sea near Cyprus, was the favorite god of sailors," he said.

The man looked contemptuous. "Venus is all very well for men of cities and women kind, but the Dioscuri is our god," and he turned away, looking as though he would like to throw Laon overboard for his ignorance.

Later in the day, when most of the work incident upon first leaving dock had been done, and the sailors were gathered in a group resting, and watching for the appearance of their favorite twin stars, one of them suddenly said,

"Ah, shipmates, ye should have been with me the last time I sailed from Sidon. It was about the roughest passage I ever had, and I've had some rough ones in my time. We had a cohort of the Roman guard on board in charge of some prisoners, and soldiers and sailors alike quailed at the violence of the storm. We boasted of being brave men all of us, but there was one prisoner on board who put us all to shame. He was calm and unmoved through it all, encouraged us to eat that we might be able to work, begged the soldiers not to shoot his fellow-prisoners, as they proposed—they would never have shot him, they had too much love and reverence for him, so that it was not for himself that he begged this favor—and did all he could to help us in every way, assuring us that if we only did our duty and trusted in God we should all be saved."

"Thou meanest the Dioscuri, the sailor's help and guiding-star?" interrupted one.

But the man shook his head. "I mean the God who made the stars, the Dioscuri, and all the host of heaven, and gave men wisdom to guide their vessels over the trackless deep by the motions of the sun and stars."

"Pallas Athene is the god of wisdom and knowledge," Laon ventured to say.

But the sailor dissented. "The God whom Paul preaches, and in whom I believe, is the God of wisdom as well as the creator of the stars," he said.

The group of men lifted their heads and looked at the bold speaker.

"Thou believest in this new God and forsakest our guiding stars!" exclaimed one.

"Shipmates, he is no new God—this great, wise, almighty Creator, who can control the sea, and say to its waves 'be still' at the prayer of his messenger."

"Did he do that?" asked one in awe-struck whisper.

The man nodded. "Nothing less than almighty power saved us from a watery grave," he said solemnly. "Our ship broke up just after we left her, but not a soul was lost. Some of us could swim, those who could not clung to boards and broken spars, and in this way all got safe to land, even as Paul said."

"And you believed this Paul to be one of the gods," said one sneeringly.

"Nay, nay, but he is a messenger from God—the only true God, who made the sea and stars as well as the dry land. Shipmates, we need a God such as this man came to declare—one who needeth not a statue or temple for his worship; for what can sailors do with either? We need a God who is at hand when the wild wind lashes the waves into fury—a God who holds the winds in his fists and the waters in the hollow of his hand."

"Then thy God doeth the work both of Æolus and Neptune," said one.

"Æolus and Neptune are but idols; there is but one God," said the man boldly.

His companions looked at each other in mute surprise. The speaker had already proved himself the most capable man on the vessel, or they might have doubted his sanity; but, as it was, they sat and listened with breathless attention to all he said.

"This God whom Paul came to make known to men is the Almighty God, who made heaven and earth and all men dwelling upon it. He hath not only made them, but redeemed them from sin and the power of evil by the death of his only Son, Jesus Christ the Lord."

"Then thou hast two gods after all," said one of the men.

But the speaker shook his head. "Not so. Christ came to make known the Father, and he who worships the Son worships the Father also, for he is the brightness of the Father's glory."

"Where is the temple of thy God," asked two or three together.

"He needeth no temple, for the heaven is his throne and the earth is his footstool, and there is no God but him."

"Then thou wouldst have us break down the altars we have always believed were sacred, and brand our fathers who worshiped these gods as worse than fools. Truly thy God is a jealous God, to claim the whole of man's worship."

"Yes, God is a jealous God," admitted the sailor. "He loveth not to see the worship that is alone due to him wasted on the shrine of a vain idol. And think ye this is strange?" he asked.

"Yes, so strange that few will embrace thy religion, although thou dost love it so much."

"Ha! I do love it," said the sailor fervently, "for this God is just suited for us who are out here at the mercy of the winds and waves, for he holds the winds and controls the waves."

"Well, thou dost certainly talk as though

thou hadst felt his power, and would have all of us do the same; and if it would content him to be worshiped with the twin stars, I, for one, would embrace this new faith."

But his companion shook his head. "Shipmates, ye that are fathers and know what it is to love your children, would ye be content with any but the *first* place in their hearts? Would it please ye to see them hug the gifts ye took home, but turn from thee the giver? It is just so with our great Father. We are his children, whether we know it or not; and he desires our love and worship, and will not give it to another."

The men were evidently puzzled, and knew not what reply to make to this; but the brave Christian, undaunted by their silence or the frowns of two or three, pressed his advantage, and with all the eloquence that enthusiasm alone can give, besought them not to turn from this God of love and mercy.

Laon sat and listened in silent wonder. Turn which way he would, he was to meet with some one who knew or had heard of this strange prisoner, Paul, and of the God whose messenger he was.

CHAPTER VIII.

AN ANCIENT DRESSING-ROOM.

VALERIA sat in her dressing-room, several female slaves around her, all engaged in some preparation for the young lady's toilet, which on this occasion did not seem to progress to her satisfaction.

"How inconvenient these Athenian rooms are!" she exclaimed petulantly; "there is far too much light here to be comfortable. Let down that curtain," she said to one of the slaves.

The crimson silk curtain was unlooped, and only a warm rosy light flooded the little room—for it was small, although much larger than the adjoining bed-room.

"I have not enjoyed my bath at all to-day through Glaucia not returning in time with those unguents," said the lady after a minute or two.

"Glaucia presumeth too much, kind mistress," said the slave who was combing her hair, and who had a special dislike to the pretty Greek girl.

"Thou thinkest so, Fulvia? Well, I certainly have taken a great liking to her, and she may have seen it."

"Yes, and she boasteth of it, and presumeth upon it, saying the noble Valeria would not do without her now, for her taste alone is consulted in the dressing-room," said Fulvia spitefully.

The lady's cheeks flushed. "Ha! so she boasteth of her classic Greek taste, does she?" and Valeria snatched up a small bunch of flowers that lay among the combs and perfumes on the dressing-table and trampled them under her feet. Glaucia had placed them there when she polished the bright steel mirror that morning, and her mistress knew it, and would fain have served every thing her hands had touched in the same way; for, in vaunting her taste, Glaucia had evidently underrated her own, her mistress thought, and this was a slight she could not endure.

She sat before a dressing-table on which her favorite waiting-maid had arranged the combs, and jewels, and ribbons to be worn that day, as well as the bright steel mirror, and cosmetics, and perfumes; while close at hand hung an amber-satin tunic and a broad pearl-studded girdle, with slippers similarly embroidered lying near, all ready for her mistress's use.

Valeria glanced at the robe angrily. "Put it aside," she said, "I shall not wear it. O dear, how thou art pulling my hair!" she exclaimed.

"I am sorry, but I fear it hath been neglected of late," said Fulvia artfully.

"Neglected! I am sure it hath not," said Valeria sharply; and the girl saw she was going a little too far in her disparagement of Glaucia's work.

"I do not mean that it hath not been duly brushed and powdered each day, but this Greek fashion that Glaucia persuades my mistress is so becoming is far less trouble than—"

"I shall not have it done the Greek fashion to-day; our own Roman style of curls is quite as good," interrupted Valeria.

A bunch of small false curls was brought and laid upon the dressing-table, and these Fulvia proceeded to weave in with her mistress's hair, so that it was impossible to tell which was false and which was real, and these small curls were raised one above another to an amazing height. Just as the last pin was adjusted Glaucia came in, looking hot and tired, with her quick walk from the market. She was surprised to see that the work of dressing her mistress had proceeded so far, and stammered out a few words of apology, looking somewhat frightened, however, as she did so.

Valeria turned and looked at her angrily. "O, thou hast come back at last!" she said. "By sweet Venus, I thought thou didst not intend returning at all," and she took up a roll of papyrus, and began reading the verses that had been sent to her by an Athenian acquaintance a short time before.

Glaucia laid aside her cloak, and, taking up the slippers, began adjusting the white thongs, ready to fasten them on her mistress's feet.

"Put them down. Fulvia will do all that is needed," said Valeria coldly when she saw Glaucia approaching.

The poor girl put aside the slippers, and although she could scarce keep back her tears, for she was really sorry that she had not been back in time to dress her mistress, she began the more lowly work of clearing away the litter for the other slaves.

But Fulvia interfered now. "Do not touch my things," she said, "for, by Ceres, I know not how I shall dress my sweet mistress to-morrow if thou dost."

"Thou mayest leave the dressing-room," said Valeria, shortly; and this permission, which was of course intended as a command, Glaucia dared not otherwise construe. She went out silently and sadly, half wishing she had not stopped to listen to the old man in the market; and yet she could not feel altogether sorry, for it was such good news for her, and Laon, and every slave in Athens.

Meanwhile Valeria was dressed according to the taste of Fulvia, which was not very likely to be at all Greek in its character, for, as she was often saying, she hated Athens and all belonging to it; and so, instead of wearing the tunic of amber that so well became her complexion, and with the plain classic banding of her hair that set off the exquisite poise of her head so effectually, the lady arrayed herself in a dress of pink and white, and with numerous pins and bands of ribbon interspersed with her curls, looked an over-dressed Roman beauty rather than an elegantly dressed lady.

Company was expected to supper that afternoon; but six or eight were considered a comfortable number for a dinner party in those days; and in Athens, where no modest woman ever appeared at an entertainment, these were strictly confined to the sterner sex.

Fabrizzio Gracchi, however, who had always been accustomed to see his wife at the table, insisted that she should not resign her place, but that Valeria should likewise sit with the company, for if ladies were present the wine did not circulate quite so freely, or the company become so boisterous, for even philosophers sometimes forgot the bounds of moderation. But, although Fabrizzio wished his daughter to appear at all the entertainments given at home, he very much disliked seeing her dressed in the present style of Roman fashion, and had commended her taste in adopting the plainer Grecian style of wearing her hair. His surprise, therefore, may be imagined when Valeria entered the gallery where he sat to receive his guests.

"My daughter, thou hast changed thy dressing-maid," said her father, looking at the ponderous pile of curls and ribbons.

Valeria, who already felt very cross at Glaucia's absence, did not want to be reminded of the fact, so she said shortly, "Yes, my father, as thou knowest, I love a change sometimes."

"But this change is not improving," observed the philosopher, a remark which Valeria chose to interpret as praise of Glaucia's taste and disparagement of her own.

She did not, however, reply to it, for at the same moment the slave in attendance drew aside the embroidered curtain that hung at the entrance, and their first visitor was announced.

Fabrizzio still clung to the old-fashioned Roman toga, but no one wishing to be thought at all stylish in their dress wore that now. The Greek tunic had replaced the toga even in Rome, and their visitor's was of the richest Tyrian dye, and fastened with buckles sparkling with emeralds. The sleeves were loose, and fringed at the wrist with gold; and a broad girdle at the waist, worked in arabesque designs, to match the sleeves, answered the double purpose of band and pockets, for in them was carried the handkerchief, purse, stylus or iron pen, and the waxen tablets.

Fabrizzio received his visitor with all the respect and courtesy of the grand old Roman time that was so rapidly passing away, and very soon they were lost in a philosophical discussion, and wandered off to the tablinum, or library, whither they were followed by other guests as they arrived.

Supper was at length announced, and a slave led the way to the triclinium, or dining-room, where couches were placed for the gentlemen to recline on during meals; but elaborately carved chairs, studded with gold and ivory, were set for the ladies. There were three tables, so placed that the guests sat on one side, and the slaves in attendance stood on the other. One side of the room was open to the peristyle, in the center of which a fountain threw up tiny jets of water, and the musical plash in the marble basin sounded delightfully cool and refreshing. Between the marble pillars that supported the roof hung baskets of the choicest flowers, while the image and shrine of Flora, which stood opposite, was wreathed with garlands, the votive offerings of Valeria and her mother. To this, their favorite goddess, the ladies bowed as they entered, as well as to the sacred lares, or household gods, placed, with the salt, at the corner of each table.

As the guests seated themselves the slaves appeared with the first course. Amid fresh figs, sweet herbs strewed with snow, eggs and anchovies, were cups of wine mixed with honey, and these were handed round by the slaves to each of the company. Fabrizzio then rose, and, bowing to the images at the corners of the table, sprinkled some of the wine, saying, "Be favorable, O Vesta!" words which always carried Valeria's thoughts back to her sister, who was dedicated to the service of this queen of the household gods.

As the first course was cleared away other slaves appeared, bearing a silver bowl of perfumed water and fringed napkins, which were handed to the company, who, after thus refreshing themselves, were ready for the next course.

The famous spiced Falernian wine was now brought on, and the host, rising and sprinkling a few drops as before, turned to the statue of the wine-god and said, "Be propitious, O Bacchus!" A Phrygian attagen, a dish of nightingales' tongues, and oysters from far-off Britain, graced this part of the feast.

Then followed sweetmeats, and drinks cooled with snow; while the sound of music was heard slowly approaching. The musicians, however, did not appear, but, stationing themselves in the adjoining gallery, played some sweet, soft airs, and after the removal of the last course, and the performance of the last lavation, several of the guests sung· and one, who was a poet, read from a roll of papyrus his last poem. Then the conversation drifted into the usual channels. Fabrizzio talked of philosophy, his wife the last Roman fashions and the splendor of the games in the arena, while Valeria was listening to the account a young Greek was giving her of the discourse in the market-place.

"We Athenians are accused of loving every novelty that comes in our way, and truly that old man's preaching was a novelty, only it was so blasphemous."

Valeria started. "Thou shouldst not have listened if our gods were insulted," she said.

"But thou seest it was something new—something altogether so novel that the temptation was altogether too strong for an Athenian to resist;" and, taking out his tablets from his girdle, he said, "See, I have been at the trouble of putting down some things this old man said."

Valeria looked at the white wax tablets curiously. "May I read them?" she asked.

"Certainly, if you can; but the stylus is somewhat out of order, and I fear you will not be able."

But Valeria slowly traced out the delicate Greek characters, and read, "There is but one true God. All the idols of the nations shall perish."

"Idols!" repeated Valeria, looking up; "what did he mean?"

"O! he left us in no doubt as to his meaning," said the young Greek lightly. "He said that Jupiter and Pallas, with Juno, and all the rest of our gods, were but vain idols."

Valeria sat and gazed at him in horror. "Is it possible there can be such wretches in the world," she said; and then, suddenly recollecting the farewell visit of their friend Julia, she exclaimed, "Why, there is a sect in Rome that proclaim the same falsehoods!"

"Ha, the Nazarenes! I have heard of them, and I doubt not this old man is of the same sect, although he calls himself a Christian, after one whom he calls the Lord Christ," replied her visitor.

"Yes, they are the same sect, I know," and she was about to say that a friend of their own had been deluded into joining them, but she reflected that to own as a friend one of these miserable people would be to incur almost lasting disgrace, so she merely said, "I heard something about them just before I left Rome."

"Indeed, what did you hear?" asked her guest. "You see I try to make a study—collect all the evidence I can—about any new startling subject like this. It is an amusement that passes away many a weary hour; for since we cannot all be philosophers, and ambition in the State is out of the question since we bowed to the mistress of nations and adopted the laws of Rome, we are glad of any new gossip, any slight change—"

"But this would be no 'slight change' if these people could have their will," interrupted Valeria, "for they would destroy our gods if they could, I doubt not."

"Yes, every statue would be broken, and every altar would be thrown down," said the young Greek coolly.

"O what impiety!" exclaimed Valeria; "truly, these people are not fit to live," she added.

"Thou wouldst have them all turned into the arena with a few tigers for company," said her guest, laughing.

"It would be the greatest kindness to the rest of mankind, for it seemeth these impious people are not content with keeping their belief or unbelief to themselves," said Valeria.

"No; they would have all men believe as they do. I never saw any one more earnest in my life than that old man in the agora to-day," he added in a more serious tone.

"How very dreadful!" said Valeria; "will not the Athenians put a stop to such doings if the prefect does not interfere?"

"You forget the Athenians love any new amusement, even to the abuse of Pallas Athene, if it can only boast of being a novelty, as this is. It is somewhat puzzling, too," he said, "for thou hast doubtless seen the altar on Mars' Hill dedicated to the Unknown God, which many suppose our great Socrates erected and worshiped at. There is no temple, no statue of this god, but the old man said it was the Unknown God who had made himself known in the person of Jesus Christ."

"Is he one of the disciples of Plato—a great and learned philosopher—this old man?" asked Valeria.

"Nay, he looks like an old slave, who has perhaps bought his liberty or had it given to him. Certainly he cannot boast of being learned."

"And the Athenians would listen to the vain babbling of an old slave," said Valeria in a tone of contempt.

"Nay, but that is the puzzle," said the Greek, "how this old man could know such things."

"He does not know them; it is but an old man's foolish tale," said Valeria. "I have learned a little of thy Plato and Socrates, and think ye that they in their wisdom would not have discovered this 'Unknown God' if he was ever to be known?"

"Plato and Socrates were certainly very wise," said the Greek.

"Yes, as wise as this old man is foolish. It is all a foolish tale—foolish and impious," decided Valeria, "and I am greatly surprised that ye Greeks do not think so."

"We do," answered the young man quickly; "but still, foolish as the whole of this religion is, it is still amusing and somewhat puzzling, and so we can afford to tolerate its votaries a little."

"But suppose with their zeal and wariness they should delude the people to believe in this impiety," said Valeria.

The young man shook his head. "They will never do that," he said; "we Greeks are too wise. This new religion, like that of Isis, will attract attention for a little while, just because it is new; but the world will never forsake the worship of Jupiter and our gods."

"Sweet Vesta, guardian of our hearths and homes, defend us from such an evil!" said Valeria devoutly; and then she went on to talk of her sister, still left in Rome to watch and wait at the sacred hearth-fire of the world, representative of every household and every heart, that they might never be forgotten by the gracious queen who presided over every household in the land.

CHAPTER IX.

THE ATHENIAN CHURCH.

AS soon as Valeria had left her dressing-room Glaucia was sent for, and told to remove her bed, and all that belonged to her, from the little room adjoining her mistress's, while Fulvia's were brought to replace them. This degradation—for it was nothing less—touched Glaucia very keenly; and when the usual slaves' room was reached she burst into a passionate flood of tears.

"I wanted to tell my mistress, too, of the strange things the old man talked of in the market-place," she sobbed, speaking softly to herself. "She is wiser than I am, and would know whether I ought to believe it, or whether he is only a deceiver; but now I have no one to talk to about it."

Between Glaucia and her fellow-slaves there had never been much companionship. Her innate refinement revolted at many things they did and said, and this, with Valeria's undisguised preference for her, had caused a feeling of bitter jealousy to spring up in their minds against her, so that, with one exception, all her companions rejoiced at her downfall; and Fulvia determined, now that she could be near her mistress again, to set her so thoroughly against Glaucia that she should never regain her lost place. She took care, too, that the work of preparing her mistress's powders and unguents should be such as to occupy Glaucia at a distance from Valeria's rooms, and that she should be sent on the different errands, so that she might never be likely to see her mistress to speak to her.

Glaucia at first was very unhappy about this, but the frequent visits she was consequently obliged to make to the market reconciled her to the altered state of things more than any thing else, for she seldom failed to see the old preacher there, and he, too, had begun to look for the gentle slave who listened with such eager, hungry eyes to the good news of salvation he had to proclaim. At length he said to her—

"My daughter, wouldst thou not like to be present at our meeting this evening? A few of the faithful followers of the Lord Jesus Christ will meet together to strengthen each other's faith and hope, and we ever gladly welcome those who are anxious to learn more of this wonderful truth; and thou art one of these, I feel certain."

"Yes," answered Glaucia, with downcast eyes, "I am anxious to learn all this wonderful Gospel can teach me; but I have been troubled of late with the thought that this knowledge is not for women—at least not for modest women," she added slowly.

The old man started, and for a moment seemed puzzled; but at length he said—

"Nay, thou needest not to fear, for this Gospel is sent to men and women alike without difference. All may *learn* its blessed truths, but all may not alike *teach* them; for our Brother Paul, having regard to the immodest women among the Athenians, who stand up in the schools and declaim aloud to all who will hear them, and who have thus made it a shame and a disgrace for women of sobriety even to learn aught but the duties of a matron—having these, I say, in his mind, and being careful that no reproach should be brought upon the Gospel through this—he has given a command, saying, 'Suffer not a woman to teach;' but he would, I know, exhort all women to learn."

Glaucia bowed her head. "I will strive to come to this meeting," she said, "if thou wilt tell me where it is. I know Athens very well, and so can doubtless find it."

"Nay, but I may not do that," said the man; "for, though I preach publicly in the market-place, the Jews among us so sorely hate this Gospel that the lives of all who love it are in danger, and therefore it is deemed prudent to keep our meeting-place a secret. If, however, thou wilt come, my wife shalt lead thee. As for myself, I deem it safer to go alone, for even while preaching I am in danger of being stoned, like our first martyr, Stephen."

Glaucia shivered. "Is there, then, such danger in following this new religion?" she asked.

"Nay, call it not new," said the old man quickly. "The God whom we serve is from everlasting to everlasting; while the idols of this city are but modern inventions, that must pass away before the power of this Gospel and the might of Jesus Christ."

As Glaucia walked home, occasionally looking at the exquisite statues and splendid temples, and thought of the old man's words, she shook her head sadly. "I cannot hope this new religion will ever gain more than the love of poor slaves like myself; for, because it comes as a message of mercy to the poor, the rich and learned will never receive it. I wonder what Laon would think if he heard these glad tidings of great joy!" and Glaucia heaved another deep sigh as she thought of her brother, and how hopeless it seemed now of their ever meeting again.

The old slave, who alone had befriended Glaucia in her late trouble and disgrace, had often tried to persuade her to go out and see her former friends in the city; but the poor girl had shrunk from walking in the streets more than she could help for fear of meeting face to face any of these acquaintances, for she had seen one or two in the Agora, and had noticed how their heads were turned aside that they might not see her, or had hastened into a booth that they might avoid speaking to her, and so she had always replied—

"No, no, I cannot go where I am not welcome, and no one wishes to see Glaucia the slave!"

Sometimes she wondered whether it was the fact of her being a slave only that made her friends so utterly discard her—whether the disgrace, whatever it was, that Laon had hinted at as connected with her mother's name, had not some weight in this matter. But whatever it was, none had ventured to befriend the orphaned girl; and so, when she went home and said she wanted to go out for an hour in the evening, her companions were all very much surprised. Her friend, however, who was the oldest slave in the house in point of service, and therefore somewhat looked up to by the rest, overruled all the objections made to this by the others.

"The girl knows the city very well, and hath friends here, and it will do her good to go out. Our noble Valeria would not object to her seeing a little change, I am sure. I will ask her by and by."

But any appeal to her mistress was just what the artful Fulvia was constantly laboring to prevent, and so she said, "There is no occasion to trouble Valeria about that insignificant slave girl, I am sure. If thou thinkest she can go about the city by herself, I suppose she can, though I should not like to do so;" and Fulvia tossed her head as she walked out into the atrium.

No one thought to ask Glaucia where she was going, and so, when the time came, she went out without fear, and found her way to the house she had been directed to call at without any difficulty. An elderly woman was already dressed in her long cloak, the ample folds of which effectually concealed her face as well as her whole figure, descending, as it did, from her head, and only leaving sufficient of her face uncovered to enable her to see.

Glaucia had not thought it necessary to put on any disguise, but the woman threw a cloak over her head before they went out, and then they silently took their way through the most unfrequented parts of the city toward the coast. Soon after the city gates were passed and they had entered the wall-begirt street, that was some five miles in length, the woman moved her cloak aside and breathed more freely.

"We shall not be likely to meet any Jews now," she said in a half whisper, and very soon she turned toward one of the houses that seemed to be falling into decay, and giving a peculiar knock at the door, sat herself down on a stone to rest and wait.

Glaucia looked up at the deserted house and the wall, some sixty feet high, which had been built in the day of the city's glory, but had proved powerless to keep out the all-conquering troops of Rome. "This place is empty," she said, shivering with fear.

But the woman shook her head, and the next minute stealthy footsteps were heard approaching the place, and two other closely enveloped figures appeared.

"Hast thou knocked, Medea?" asked the elder of the two, looking closely at Glaucia as she spoke.

"Yes, most noble Damaris, I doubt not the door will be opened as soon as they have ascertained that we are friends."

"Thy husband still preaches boldly in the market-place, I see. Truly he is a brave soldier of the Lord Jesus Christ."

"We are but a feeble band here in Athens," said Medea, "and so it behoveth all who can speak to do so, especially those who heard our Brother Paul himself, and learned the truth from his lips. Only thou and Dionysius, the Areopagite, are left as fruits of his ministry, except my husband," said Medea.

"Nay, nay, thou knowest not how many of the Lord's hidden ones are dwelling with us here in Athens," said Damaris cheerfully.

"They are unworthy the name of Christ if they come not forward and declare their love for him. Nay, nay, noble Damaris, seek not to excuse their cowardice—" At this moment the heavy door was slowly swung back, and the whole party entered.

They followed their guide through several large deserted chambers to one partly underground and at the back of the building, where, as the door opened, they were each in turn greeted with the salutation, "Peace be with thee!"

The women bowed, in silent acknowledgment of the greeting, but a man who had entered just after them returned it with the words, "Peace be to all the faithful!"

The chamber was dimly lighted from a small lamp fixed in the wall, and Glaucia could see there were about a dozen people already assembled, sitting in silent thought, apparently waiting for some one else to appear. At length the door opened again, and this time a venerable-looking man, pausing on the threshold, lifted his hands and said, "Peace be to the Church of our Lord Jesus Christ!"

A fervent "Amen" was breathed by all present, and then the new-comer stepped into the middle of the chamber, and, saying a few words to Medea's husband, took a roll of papyrus from his girdle.

"This is the copy of a letter from our Brother Paul to the Church of Ephesus," he said, unrolling the papyrus. "He is still imprisoned at Rome, waiting for his trial before Nero, but is allowed to receive all who wish to visit him, none hindering him from preaching the Gospel, for which he is in bonds. These letters he desires the angels of the Churches to read aloud, and likewise to send faithful copies to all the brethren round about, and thus, as the angel of this Church, I have received it from the angel of the Church at Ephesus."

After this explanation he read Paul's greeting, addressed not only to the Ephesian Church but to "all the faithful in Christ Jesus," so that the little company at Athens could feel they had a share in the greeting, although the letter was not sent direct to them. Slowly and clearly, with the purest Greek enunciation, did the minister read through the first part of the epistle, and Glaucia sat and listened with rapt attention to those wonderful words, so new, so strange, so altogether unlike any thing she had heard before concerning the popular gods of Athens:—

"Having predestinated us unto the adoption of children by Jesus Christ to himself, according to the good pleasure of his will. . . . In whom we have redemption through his blood, the forgiveness of sins, according to the riches of his grace."

These were the words that the reader afterward rendered into more simple language, suited to the capacity of Glaucia and several others of the company.

"It is now ten years since this message was first brought to our city by this noble messenger of the then Unknown God, our Brother

Paul. It was delivered first to the Jews in their synagogue, and afterward in the market, where, as ye know, he was accused, like our philosopher Socrates, of setting forth strange gods, and might, like him, have been condemned to drink the fatal hemlock by the court of the Areopagus, before which he was brought, and to the members of which he so boldly preached the Gospel.

"O, my friends, never shall I forget the day when I was summoned to take the rock-hewn seat of judgment with other noble citizens of Athens, to hear what this 'vain babbler'—as he was called—had to say about this new divinity. I was very angry that any should question the claims of our Jupiter and Juno; but as he went on to speak of the death of the Lord Jesus Christ, and the signs in heaven that had followed it, as well as his resurrection, I could no longer resist the conviction that he was indeed the messenger of a God greater than Jupiter. I too had witnessed the things he spoke of. The supernatural darkness at midday had extended even to Heliopolis, in Egypt, and when I saw it, I exclaimed, 'Either the God of nature suffers, or the frame of the world will be dissolved!'

"I was a young man when this happened, but

I had never forgotten it, and it returned to my mind that day; and proud philosopher as I was, sitting in judgment upon this messenger, I became a learner and believer in Christ, and have since sought, as far as I could, to follow in the footsteps of my great master, Paul."

The speaker had been away from Athens, and, now that he had returned, he saw some fresh faces among his congregation besides Glaucia's, and so, for the sake of these, he spoke minutely of himself, lest they should think he had taken the pre-eminence as the minister of the Church merely on account of his superior rank.

Glaucia sat and listened in wondering amazement, gazing at the speaker with widely-dilated eyes that could see nothing else but that calm, grand, majestic face that ten years ago had been seen among the Areopagites. Truly, this religion was a marvelous one, to come with a message to slaves, inviting them to accept the redemption that had been paid for them—terms which they, as slaves, might be glad to accept; but, for this proud philosopher of the very highest rank among the citizens of Athens, how he could stoop to accept the same terms, so humbling to his pride, and become a lowly follower of the Saviour, was the puzzle.

The very name, "Saviour," was revolting to

Greek pride, she knew; and yet he had conquered it all, and gloried in the name of "Christian," and called these slaves who were present his brethren. Beyond the fact of some others being slaves, Glaucia knew nothing, saw nothing of the congregation, for as soon as Dionysius had done speaking she whispered to Medea—

"I must go now, or they will not let me come again."

"Thou wilt come again, then," said Medea quickly.

"Yes, indeed, if I am welcome," said Glaucia.

"Welcome! Nay, we are anxious that all should learn the truth, and, forsaking their idols, cleave to the Lord our God."

"Forsaking their idols!" repeated Glaucia; "what dost thou mean?"

"That none can serve the Lord Jesus Christ, and accept the redemption he has paid, unless they give up the vain worship of the idols he hates."

"But cannot I serve God—pray to him, as I have begun to do—unless I leave off weaving garlands for Pallas Athene, and pouring out a libation to Vesta and the lares?" asked Glaucia slowly and sadly.

"No, indeed, thou canst not," said the matron; "thou must choose between Pallas Athene and the Lord Jesus Christ, for thou mayest not serve both."

They had left the house while speaking; and now, having gained the gate of the city, and Medea being about to leave her, Glaucia lifted her troubled face, and said—

"I know not what I shall do; wilt thou pray for me?"

"Yes, dear child, and, what is better, the Lord will help thee," said Medea; and with these words she left her to return home alone, for if they were again seen together it might excite suspicion against Glaucia, for it was already known in Athens that Medea and her husband, as well as Damaris and Dionysius, were of the hated sect of the Nazarenes.

CHAPTER X.

THE WORSHIP OF THE GODS.

WHEN Glaucia reached home she hurried in without once raising her eyes to the garland that hung over the door, or pausing to invoke the lares as she crossed the threshold. On her way to the atrium she had to pass the statues of Flora and Vesta, but she did so without the customary reverence, for she was anxious to reach her own room, where she might sit down and think over all she had heard, especially the last words that had been spoken by Medea at the gate of the city.

She had ventured to kneel down and pray to this " Unknown God," who had neither temple nor statue in Athens, for none of the Olympian deities who were worshiped here would help Laon any more than they did her, as he was poor and friendless. But the God who was willing to be the God of slaves, willing to be her God and Father, would be equally ready to help Laon, she argued, and so for him, her beloved brother, she had prayed again and again, although for herself she had not the courage to offer a single petition.

Now, however, that Medea had told her that she must entirely renounce the worship of Pallas Athene and all her former deities, she knew not what to do—what to think. They would not help Laon; but might they not, in their anger, injure him if she failed to propitate them—failed to offer her customary service? To others these statues of marble, ivory, and gold might be idols, but to Glaucia they were very real—very terrible in their anger, when she thought of Jupiter forging thunderbolts to hurl at her defenseless brother for her neglect of service.

Thinking thus, and not feeling quite sure that she could give up the service of her old gods all at once, however much she might wish to serve the Lord, the hours passed slowly away while she lay tossing sleeplessly on her little bed.

The old slave, who shared Glaucia's room with her, lay listening to the girl's deep-drawn sighs, wondering not a little what it could be that troubled her, and resolving to speak to Valeria the next day on behalf of her former favorite, for she doubted not the artful Fulvia had again been doing something to annoy her.

This resolution, however, was forgotten the

next morning, for Pan himself seemed to have descended upon the usually quiet household, and created such a state of confusion that no one seemed to know what they were about. For some time Glaucia joined in the running backward and forward with the other slaves, but could not understand what had caused so much bustle and confusion.

At length, however, she heard that a messenger had arrived from Rome at daybreak bringing the sad news that Claudia, the vestal, was dangerously ill, and desired to see her father.

Fabrizzio was of course about to set off on his journey at once, and his slaves were doing all they could to help forward the preparation for his departure, for his wife and daughter could do nothing but lament aloud the cruelty of the Fates in ordering this just after they had left Rome.

Fabrizzio himself, although he tried to subdue all outward signs of emotion, as became a philosopher and a stoic, was, nevertheless, deeply moved at the sight of his wife's grief, but he positively refused to allow her to accompany him to Rome.

"Nay, nay, my Romola, I cannot allow thee to return at this season," said her husband firmly; "thou art not strong, and the damps of our Roman climate at this time will do thee much harm, even if thou dost not take the sickness which hath fallen upon our Claudia."

"Thou wilt bring her home, then, for me to nurse," said his wife tearfully.

But Fabrizzio looked doubtful. "Why, Romola, thou dost forget she is a vestal," he said.

"She was my child before she was the servant of Vesta," cried the mother passionately. "O, Fabrizzio, bring her back until she is restored to health! She cannot perform her duties in the temple if she is ill, and the Senate would not object to her being restored to her mother for a short time."

"Thou speakest of the Senate, but, my wife, thou dost forget the gods," said Fabrizzio seriously.

Romola hid her face in her hands for a few minutes, and when she lifted it again to her husband's it was as white and rigid as the marble Juno opposite.

"Fabrizzio, I will brave the anger of the gods," she said in a whisper. "Bring my child home or I shall die!"

Her husband saw it would be useless to discuss this point with her, and so he said, "I will dispatch a messenger to thee bearing tidings of Claudia's state as soon as I reach Rome. Are the slaves ready?" he asked.

Again the mother's grief and anxiety overcame every other feeling. "O Claudia, Claudia, my child! shall I ever see thee again? wilt thou ever recover from this sickness?" she exclaimed, wringing her hands in hopeless grief.

The freedman, who came in at this moment to say the slaves and mules were ready to start, looked pityingly at the lady. "The Delphic Oracle might be consulted for the relief of the noble Romola," he suggested.

The lady heard the words, and caught at once at the suggestion. "Valeria and a few slaves could go with me," she said eagerly.

Fabrizzio looked perplexed. "Thou art forgetful of the dangers of such a journey, my Romola," he said.

"The messenger who hath just arrived from Rome traveled with messengers from the emperor and Senate, and when their letters to the Prefect of Athens are delivered they are to journey to Corinth to consult the Oracle of the gods of Delphi concerning the late troubles in Britain, and the noble Romola might join their cavalcade and thus travel in safety," said the freedman.

"Certainly, that might be done," said Fabrizzio musingly; "but what is the Oracle to be consulted upon? Are you sure these messengers are going to Corinth or Delphi?" he asked.

"Yes; the emperor is anxious to know whether the barbarian islanders will ever be entirely conquered. Their queen, Boadicea, has been defeated, it is true; but Camulodunum, (Colchester,) Verulamium, (St. Albans,) and Londinium, (London,) have been burned to ashes, and seventy thousand of our people in these colonies have perished."

"And our Nero is so occupied with amusing the people with his performances as an actor that he intends to give up this mighty undertaking, which cost our Cæsar so much, and for which our great road through Gaul was constructed," said Fabrizzio contemptuously. "But I forget—time wears, and I may not stay gossiping with thee, Anicetus. Let every thing be prepared for this journey to Delphi, and do thou go thyself to command the slaves, and take charge of my Romola;" saying which the philosopher and his wife passed out of the atrium into a little side room to bid each other farewell, for this journey was beset by so many perils that they might never meet again.

They each tried to speak cheerfully and hopefully now that the moment of parting had come, but it was an utter failure on the part of the lady, and Fabrizzio was obliged to tear himself away, leaving her fainting in the arms of her attendant slaves, whom he had summoned.

As the philosopher, with his numerous lictors, slaves, and freedmen, wended their way slowly through the gate of the city toward the Piræus, Romola was slowly recovering from her swoon. Valeria was standing by her mother's side when she opened her eyes, and to her the lady turned instinctively for comfort.

"My Valeria, I shall never see him again. My Fabrizzio and Claudia are both summoned to the all-embracing arms of Mars. Would that the goddess could be appeased with a less costly treasure, or that we knew more of the Elysian fields that await us beyond—could be quite sure that there is an Elysium beyond the funeral urn! for this is by no means certain, it seems, since our wisest philosophers know not whether it is a fable or a truth;" and the lady heaved a deep sigh as she spoke.

Valeria wished she could speak words of comfort confidently, and assure her mother there was another life beyond the tomb; but though she and her father were both studying the writings of the wisest men in Greece to ascertain this point, it was by no means clear to them yet. She knew well, too, the danger her father was likely to encounter in going to Rome at this unhealthy season of the year, when the malaria-laden breezes from the marshes of the Tiber carried disease and death to so many in the Imperial City. All who were able to do so left at this season, and retired to Pompeii or Herculaneum. Nero himself had a most gorgeous palace at the former place, and all fashionable Rome flocked after their emperor when he left the city, so that it would be almost deserted at this time by all but the poorest, and those who, like Claudia, were compelled to stay behind.

This was an additional anxiety to Valeria and her mother, but they resolved to send a sacrifice at once to the shrine of Hygeia. The goddess was often neglected, and almost forgotten, until sickness entered the family; but they hoped she was not so deeply offended that she would not restore her precious gift of health to Claudia, or withhold it from Fabrizzio. Talking of this, and carefully abstaining from any mention of the capriciousness of their gods, Valeria at last succeeded in soothing her mother, while Anicetus made preparations for their instant departure from Athens to join the imperial cavalcade.

Greatly to the annoyance of Fulvia, Glaucia

was told to prepare herself for this journey, as well as the old slave who had been so long the faithful attendant of Romola; and, after issuing this command, Valeria went, as was her custom, to the shrine of Flora, expecting to see it decked with fresh flowers as usual, for this was not only Glaucia's duty, but her delight, and had never before been neglected. But, to Valeria's surprise and anger, the withered flowers of the previous day had not been removed, and not a fresh one was to be seen.

"Why is this, Felicita?" she angrily demanded, turning to the old slave, who happened to be passing through the peristyle; and, pointing to the untidy-looking shrine, Valeria said, "Send Glaucia to me; it is her duty to place fresh flowers here."

"Doubtless it hath been forgotten in the hurry and confusion this morning," said Felicita by way of excuse.

"But the shrine of our goddess should be more carefully tended than ever, now that we are in trouble," said Valeria. "Send Glaucia to me at once!"

The poor girl came forward a few minutes afterward trembling with fear, not so much at the thought of her mistress's anger, as that of the goddess whose service she had willfully

Glaucia Reproved for Neglecting the Shrine of Flora.

neglected, for it was not through forgetfulness the shrine had remained untended this morning. The look of consternation and fright in the poor girl's face was so visible that Valeria would not scold her, however, as she had intended.

"I see thou art conscious of thy fault and sorry for it too, Glaucia, and doubtless our gracious Flora will forgive it this once, as I do, but never let it occur again or I—" Valeria did not say what she would do, but the look that accompanied the words was in itself so threatening that Glaucia shivered with unknown terror. "Now go and gather fresh flowers while I remove these faded ones," she added, and as she spoke the proud patrician lady kneeled down and carefully removed every faded leaf from the marble pedestal, while Glaucia went hastily to the garden, and, with trembling fingers, pulled the first flowers she saw, without regard to the purpose for which they were needed.

Half blinded with tears, the poor girl raised her streaming eyes to the cloudless blue of the morning skies, and exclaimed, "I have done it! I have offended the great God by gathering these for Flora, and he will not help Laon!" and she sobbed forth her grief and wrung her hands in the anguish of her soul.

She could not long indulge in this outburst, for her mistress was waiting, she knew, in the peristyle, so she hastily collected what she had gathered and hurried back with them.

The lady frowned as she looked at them. "Thou art very careless this morning, Glaucia," she said severely. "There is not a flower here worthy of our goddess; thou hast gathered the most worthless rubbish our garden will produce instead of the most costly."

The color deepened in Glaucia's cheeks, but she did not reply. In truth she did not know what she had gathered until she began to help her mistress to arrange them; and then she too saw that they were almost useless.

"It is well thou art coming with us on our journey to Delphi, or I fear that not only would the shrine of Flora be neglected, but even the customary offerings to our lares would also be forgotten if left to thy care," said the lady in a tone of displeasure.

It was the first intimation Glaucia had received of this journey, for Fulvia had not yet told her of her mistress's command; but she did not feel sorry when she knew that they were to join the Roman guard of the emperor. They had just come from Rome, and she had left Laon there, and, unlikely as it seemed, they might have heard something about him. She ventured to mention her hopes to her friend, Felicita, while they were preparing to depart, but the old slave shook her head.

"I greatly fear thou wilt never hear of thy brother again," she said sadly.

Glaucia's face grew ashy white, and forgetting every thing else in her love for her brother, she said, "Tell me what thou meanest! Dost thou think the great God is so very angry about the flowers that he will not let me see Laon now?"

"Tush, child! the gods cannot be troubled with the sorrows of slaves," said the woman impatiently.

"No, not our gods who dwell on Olympus, but the great God who made heaven and earth—the God of all men, slave and freeborn, he cares for poor Laon."

The woman looked at her in open-eyed wonder. "What art thou talking of, child?" she said. "There is no god so poor that he will care for slaves," she said.

"No, he is not poor, but rich, and he loves us so much that he gave his Son, Jesus Christ, to die for us," said Glaucia quickly.

But before she had finished speaking the woman had seized her by the arm, and looked at her with dilating eyes. "Dost thou know what thou art talking about, child?" she asked in a hoarse whisper. "Where didst thou meet with these wicked Nazarenes, these atheists, who say there is no God?"

"Nay, if the old man who preaches in the market is a Nazarene he is not wicked, nor does he say there is no God, for he tells of One greater than our Jupiter, and kinder than Juno or our Pallas Athene," said Glaucia warmly.

"And thou hast been listening to him—that old Nazarene who preaches in the market. I see it now; thy neglect of Flora's shrine was willful, and thou too art half a Nazarene. O wretched, miserable girl! what thy fate will be when the noble Valeria hears it I tremble to think."

Glaucia turned pale and trembled too, but still she did not lose her courage entirely. "My mistress will not be so very angry when she hears that this God is the only one for slaves."

"Angry, girl? Thou dost not know Valeria if thou thinkest she will forgive any slight to the gods. Forget what thou hast heard in the market, it will be easy to do so, since thou wilt not go there again for some time. This journey to Delphi too will help thee, and I will keep thy secret, so that no harm is done if thou dost not tell that artful Fulvia about it."

"I will not tell Fulvia about it, but I cannot forget what I have learned," said Glaucia, her eyes slowly filling with tears as she spoke. "Felicita, I have prayed to this great God for my brother Laon, and I know he will hear me, and let me see him once more," and the poor girl smiled triumphantly through her tears.

CHAPTER XI.

THE DELPHIC ORACLE.

ROMOLA and Valeria reclined in their litter, around which were drawn curtains of embroidered silk to shut out the inquisitive gaze of foot passengers, and leave the ladies free to indulge their grief or converse upon the slender hope they had of Claudia's recovery. Immediately in front of them Anicetus drove in a chariot of bronze, upon the sides of which were wrought in relief the Olympian games, for, as the representative of Fabrizzio, he would travel in the same state as his master; and the train was now headed by his chariot, drawn by two horses of the rarest breed of Parthia, whose fiery speed could with difficulty be brought down to the pace of the lictors, who walked before to clear the road of all obstacles.

Behind the litter of the ladies came their female slaves and one or two Greek clients, who had placed themselves under Fabrizzio's protection since he had been at Athens, and who had volunteered to accompany Romola to point out the best roads to be taken on their journey. They took the road leading to the Marathon gate of the city, which led them through the most fashionable streets of Athens, where their progress was necessarily very slow, for, in spite of the lictors, some part of the train was constantly being separated from the rest by the rapidly driven car of some fashionable young Greek, whose exquisitely poised limbs, as he stood with the reins gathered tightly in his hands, were not unapt models of Phœbus himself.

At the portico of the temple of Fortuna there was a general halt, while Anicetus went in to place incense on the sacred tripod, and sacrifice to the blind goddess on behalf of his mistress for the success of their journey, and then the cavalcade wound slowly on past the gayly decorated open shops, the sparkling fountains that at every vista threw up their cooling spray in the summer air, the crowds of elegantly-robed loungers and bustling slaves pacing to and fro with large bronze buckets on their heads, the tiny, exquisite gardens, where they caught gleams of white marble and saw the sacred tripod that brought to Glaucia's mind her trouble more vividly than ever. But for these gardens, and their elegant reminders of what the poor girl would fain have forgotten, for a short time she might have been as gay as Fulvia herself, for it was impossible for a Greek to resist all these influences of brightness, beauty, and gushing, brimming life by which they were surrounded.

When the city gates were passed, and the streets Glaucia knew so well had been left behind, they pushed on more rapidly along the country road. Quite as beautiful was the scene spread before them here. In the distance rose the snow-crowned Hymettus, its sides covered with the chestnut, ilex, cypress, and plane trees, that grow so luxuriantly in that climate; while all along the road were copses of olive, fig, and pomegranate trees, interspersed with green meadows, guarded by myrtle and oleander hedges, or fallow fields, where the corn had been cut in May, and where mint, thyme, and rosemary were now springing up among less noxious weeds.

There were fewer statues of Venus to be seen in this country district. Ceres, with her bunch of grain, was the favorite deity of the farmers; and the hideous half-man half-goat statue of Pan was set up for the shepherds and bee-keepers; while Pallas Athene, in her character of light-giver, and Jupiter, as the father of gods and men, shared with these favorite deities the veneration of the country people.

Glaucia had heard of all these, but with Pan and Ceres, as well as many others, she had nothing to do; and when she thought of the great God combining all the attributes of all the gods in himself, and exercising all their care and power, it seemed something too wonderful for comprehension, and she bowed her head in instinctive awe at the thought.

But the god each had been told to propitiate and sacrifice to above all others was Mercury, for he must bear the message from the gods that would relieve their anxiety or plunge them into deeper gloom; he must inspire the lips of the oracle at Delphi, and as none of their deities were remarkable for their truth, Mercury might bear a false message if not propitiated. So at each of the principal temples of Mercury on their route incense was offered to that god.

The Roman cavalcade had joined them soon after leaving the gate of Athens, and as they wished to push on to Corinth as quickly as possible, there was only time for Anicetus to perform this duty, as he could drive more rapidly in his chariot than the whole cavalcade could travel. At last, after two days' weary march, the temple of Venus, crowning the lofty rock

Acrocorinthus, two thousand feet above the sea, burst upon their view. Here they would rest for a day, while their Roman companions transacted their business, before going the remaining forty miles to Delphi.

Corinth was as unlike Athens as a modern city full of bustle and mercantile business is unlike an ancient seat of learning, where art and science are almost the sole study and occupation of its inhabitants. Neptune here occupied the place of Pallas Athene, but a statue of bronze had been erected to her in the market-place scarcely less splendid than that of the Acropolis at Athens. Nor were the temples less splendid or numerous, while in addition to the gods and heroes was a long line of statues and busts erected along the road to the honor of the victors of the Isthmian games, celebrated here every year, and attracting hundreds of visitors to this, the most famous city of Greece for pleasure and luxury.

To our visitors, however, there was little to attract, and they were anxious to reach their destination as soon as possible, where they hoped the terrible suspense which they now endured would be at an end. Of course, they would have to wait until the more important communication affecting the distant barbarian island was given;

but, Mercury being favorable, they hoped they should not be kept waiting for their message.

The next forty miles, after leaving Corinth, was almost entirely across a level stretch of country, and so was passed in a shorter time than the former part of the journey. Here, too, they could hope to rest awhile and recruit their strength before commencing their home ward march.

Romola and Valeria both needed rest, but scarcely so much as their slave, Glaucia, who was almost exhausted with the fatigue of this long journey. Now, however, she could rest, and the necessity for this spared her the pain of attending her mistress to the various temples, and sacrificing to the gods while waiting for the utterance of the renowned Oracle.

At length, however, the important day arrived when the Oracle was to be consulted, and the whole family went up to the temple to wait, in reverent silence, while Anicetus drew near with the priest to listen to the sacred words that should bring weal or woe to his mistress. When at last the silence was broken, however, the message was so enigmatical that it brought but little comfort to the anxious travelers:

"The reaper gathereth not flowers, but ripened corn, with his sickle."

This trite saying was all the Oracle could be induced to utter, and with this they were obliged to commence their return journey, after spending nearly a week in Delphi. Toward the end of the second day's march, as they drew near the gates of Corinth, Glaucia was taken ill, and her illness increased so rapidly that it was deemed advisable to leave her behind at Corinth, in the care of the old slave Felicita. Lodgings were taken for them by Anicetus in a humble quarter of the town, for living was so expensive here that a fortune might soon be spent if no care were used; indeed, it was a common proverb at this time, "Not every man can go to Corinth."

Anicetus had had some difficulty in finding any one who would take the two slaves under their roof; but at last a poor widow, who got her living by sewing at the rough hair-cloth manufactured in the looms here, consented to take Glaucia and her nurse into her house, and here they were left while the rest went on to Athens.

The widow's house at Corinth was very different from the patrician house at Athens—a small hall or atrium, and two tiny bedrooms on one side of it, composed the whole; but it was not the smallness of the house that struck Felicita as being so peculiar, as its want of every thing considered so essential in other houses, even the poorest. In the center of the atrium stood the impluvium, or reservoir for rain water —for this tiny hall was open to the sky, like those of the wealthier dwellings—but there was not a statue or image to be seen, not the faintest attempt to present the household gods for worship. In vain Felicita looked in every corner of the atrium and little bedroom; nothing was seen of the lares and penates, nor was there any image of Venus or Juno.

Felicita ventured to tell Glaucia of this when they were left to themselves at night, for she was very much shocked at what seemed to her the atheism this bespoke.

"Glaucia, it is dreadful," she said, "to think that our Juno, the queen of heaven and goddess of married women, should not even have an image in this house."

"But perhaps the woman does not worship our gods," said Glaucia wearily.

"Does not worship our gods!" repeated Felicita. "What dost thou mean? Surely, thou art not thinking she is an atheist—one of those hateful Nazarenes!"

"I can't think of any thing; I only want to go to sleep," said the girl, lying down on the little mattress as she spoke.

"If I thought she was one of these Nazarenes I would not stay in the house a single night," said Felicita; "I would even now go after Anicetus and—" but a deep groan from Glaucia interrupted her, and the household gods as well as the national deities were alike forgotten, and she was glad to accept the services of the widow, who offered to prepare some herb-tea for the sick girl; for instead of going to sleep, as she said, Glaucia lay tossing restlessly on the bed, sometimes groaning with pain, and at times delirious.

The next day she was more quiet, but did not seem much better, and Felicita was glad to see the widow bring her coarse, rough sewing into the atrium, for kindness is stronger than any creed; and, in spite of her atheism, Felicita's heart was drawn toward the woman who had befriended them. The widow had not been at work long, however, before a visitor came in, a delicate-looking, plainly-dressed woman, who seated herself by the widow, and bade her go on with her work.

"So thou hast two visitors, I hear?" she said in a gentle, musical voice. "That they are poor and needy I need not ask; but are they sisters from another Church?"

"Nay, I know not that, but they are slaves,

and one is sick, and none would take them in," said the widow.

"And thou, mindful of the example of Him, our Master, who went about doing good both to the bodies and souls of men, hast taken these poor wayfarers under thy roof. That thou canst do, and we will not grudge thee the privilege; but the Church must help thee in the rest, for thou hast neither food nor raiment to spare."

"It is not food or raiment they need, noble Hyrmina, but shelter only, for they are the slaves of a wealthy Roman family, whose freed-man brought them hither."

"Because one was sick, thou sayest. Well, suffer her not to want any thing in her sick-ness that the Church can supply. Our Sister Phœbe will visit thee if I do not come again; but should any need arise thou hadst better send to me, as my house is at hand."

The visitor then drew a papyrus-roll from her girdle and read to the astonished ears of Felicita a wonderful account of a starving mul-titude being fed with five loaves and two small fishes.

"It was a God, and not a man, who could do such a work as that!" exclaimed the slave, half aloud, as she sat within her little room listening.

"It is sweet to know the Lord Christ cared even that his people should have daily bread," said the widow as the papyrus was rolled up again.

"Yes, and he has promised to reward even the cup of cold water given for his sake, and so we should be thankful for the opportunity of administering to the necessity of strangers as well as saints," said the visitor as she rose to leave.

How strange it all sounded to Felicita, who sat listening close by. These people worshiped a God who, unlike Jupiter and the rest of the Olympian deities, took care of his worshipers, noting even their smallest acts, instead of being taken up with his own pleasure and amusement. She would have liked to talk to Glaucia about this, but the poor girl was unable to converse.

As the days passed, instead of getting better she grew worse, and living in Corinth being very expensive, the sum of money Anicetus had left them was exhausted, and the widow was compelled to ask for some help to keep her lodgers from starving, as well as a change of linen for Glaucia.

"Thy wants will all be supplied, for what the chief deaconess of our Church, Phœbe, cannot give me from the treasury, will be supplied by the other, Hyrmina, for she holdeth that her riches should be divided between the poorer brethren, even as it is in some of the Churches."

"My master, who is a noble Roman, will repay thy Church for the care of us," said Felicita.

"Nay, nay, but we look not for payment," said the widow. "It is true, we are not rich in this world's goods, but our God will never suffer us to want. He is the Lord of heaven and earth, and can supply all our need, and will do it, that we may minister to others."

Certainly Glaucia had no need to complain of the ministering. Had she been in her master's house she could not have had her wants better supplied; and as for tendance, the widow came to sit with her whenever Felicita was obliged to leave, for the fever ran high, and she could not be left alone.

Hyrmina, the deaconess, sent an ample supply of clothes and linen, and called every day, bringing grapes and pomegranates and pleasant snow-cooled drinks, but she never came beyond the entrance to the atrium now, and rarely stopped five minutes with the widow. Felicita wished she would read again from the strange roll, but it had never been produced since, and she heard her say one day,

"I dare not linger long for fear this poor girl's sickness should be infectious, and I should take it to others whom I visit."

What had brought on the attack the physician could not tell, but he forbade any one talking to her, and so the weary days passed on, until at length the fever had run its course, and she began to get better. Her kind friend, the deaconess, to whom she owed her life—for she it was who brought the physician, and sent all that was necessary for her during her illness—had been afraid to see her while she was so ill, and now that she began to get better and desired to thank one who had done so much for a friendless stranger, she heard, to her disappointment, that she now had been seized with a sudden illness. It was not fever, though, but a weakness to which she was subject, and which had been brought on by trouble years before.

"Nay, but the gentle lady whom I heard reading to you surely cannot have suffered from any trouble," said Felicita.

"She hath suffered very sorely I have heard; nay, it hath cost her more than life itself to serve the Lord Christ faithfully," said the widow.

"And this Christ is your God, and you are of this sect called Nazarenes," said the slave quickly.

"Nay, we are called Christians, as we strive to follow in the footsteps of Christ," said the widow.

"Christians or Nazarenes, I will not speak against ye again," said Felicita warmly; "and I hope this deaconess will soon be better, that we may see her before we return to Athens."

It had caused Felicita some uneasiness that no tidings had come from there, since they did not return at the time they were to do so; but now Anicetus, coming to ascertain the cause of their delay, arrived too soon, for he came before Hyrmina could leave the house, or even see visitors, and so Glaucia was obliged to return to Athens without once seeing her friend.

CHAPTER XII.

DECISION.

ANICETUS brought bad news with him to Corinth. His master had returned from Rome bringing Claudia with him, but he was so ill that their friend Julia and one of her slaves had accompanied him back, and they were both at Athens still.

Felicita had heard of Julia's change of faith—had heard her called a Nazarene by Romola, and she wondered whether it was this new, strange faith that gave her courage to brave the pestilence, for it was this from which Claudia had been suffering, and her father had taken it likewise. So destitute were they of all help, notwithstanding their wealth, that but for Julia's energetic kindness they must have perished; for every one but she and a faithful slave had refused to go near the stricken father and his daughter.

"This slave is a blind Jewess too," said Anicetus when he was relating the account, "and devotedly fond of her mistress."

"And Claudia is better, say you?"

"Certainly she is, for if the pestilence had not left her she could not have come to Athens," said Anicetus.

"And my master is better?" inquired Glaucia.

"The gods defend us from such a sickness as he has had. I fear he will never be better until he reaches the abode of the shades," said Anicetus with a sigh.

Felicita shivered. An intimation, even, of death was always shrank from, for there was such an uncertainty hanging over the dark future that none knew what to hope or what to believe.

Glaucia would have preferred to tell them what she had heard of that future life, but she had not the courage yet; and besides, she hardly knew herself what to believe of tidings so wonderful—of a message sent to slaves concerning matters that their deepest thinking and most devout philosophers had failed to penetrate.

When Athens was at length reached she found that she was to resume her personal attendance on Valeria, while Fulvia waited on Claudia and their guest, for the blind girl was not able to do all that was required of a lady's maid.

They had traveled by slow and easy stages to Athens, so that Glaucia's strength was now almost entirely restored, and she was able to resume her duties as soon as she reached home, and one of the first of these was to decorate the shrine of Flora.

Slowly and hesitatingly she went to the garden in search of the asphodel and iris her mistress commanded her to gather, for her faith in the God of the Christians had grown stronger, and she was more than ever convinced that she ought not to join in the worship of these false gods any longer. But how could she tell her mistress of this change of faith? She had learned to love her, and this made it far more difficult to do any thing likely to displease her. The punishment that might be inflicted, the disgrace that would follow her declaration, were not thought of; the question had narrowed itself down to this, which was the stronger, her love to Christ or love to her mistress?

At last she laid down the flowers she was gathering and resolutely turned toward the house. "The Lord Christ will help me," she said, and she turned toward the peristyle, where she knew that her mistress was then sitting with her sister and their guest. The lady looked surprised to see her slave enter empty-handed, and she said quickly,

"Glaucia, thou art ill again!"

But Glaucia shook her head. "No, I am not ill," she said, trying to speak steadily, "but I cannot weave garlands for the gods now."

Valeria started. "Cannot weave garlands for our Flora!" she exclaimed. "And wherefore art thou thus disobedient?"

"Because—because I have learned to love the Lord Jesus Christ," said Glaucia in a trembling whisper.

Valeria started to her feet as though a serpent had stung her. "Slave! dost thou know what thou art saying? dost thou dare to come to me and say thou wilt not worship the gods of Rome, and thine own native Athene?"

Lower and lower drooped Glaucia's head, while her tears fell upon the mosaic pavement, and for a minute or two she could not reply for the sobs that shook her slight frame; but at length she ventured to raise her eyes to her mistress's angry face.

"I am sorry, so sorry to displease thee, but I cannot worship our false gods again, for I have learned to know that there is but one true God," she said.

"And where didst thou learn this?" asked her mistress. "Tell me, and I will punish these people as well as thee," she added, and she glanced at Julia as she spoke.

The lady, however, although she looked pityingly at Glaucia, could not be accused of teaching her this Christian faith, for there had not been either time or opportunity for her to do it, however willing, or even anxious, she might be to impart her knowledge to others.

Glaucia, however, did not answer her mistress, and she repeated her question, commanding her to reply immediately.

"I cannot tell thee who taught me," she said; "but I thought thou wouldst be glad to hear there was a religion for slaves."

"Ah! truly, this Christian religion is only fit for slaves and malefactors, for the God they worship was crucified—died the death of a slave and malefactor."

"But he rose again from the dead, and thus proved himself greater than all the gods of Rome by bringing life and immortality to light," said Julia quickly.

Glaucia glanced toward the lady, and silently thanked her with her eyes for thus defending their faith.

Again Valeria commanded the girl to tell her who had taught her these things, but she again refused to do this.

"I will bear any punishment, but I cannot tell thee this," she said firmly.

The lady, finding she could not extort this information from her at present, dismissed her, and then, turning to her sister, asked what she ought to do in the matter. Claudia had taken no part in the discussion before, and, now that she was appealed to, a deep color stole into her pale face, and she glanced at Julia as she said,

"What ought I to say, Julia?"

But the lady only shook her head, while the color went and came in Claudia's face so quickly that Valeria was puzzled to understand what this strange manner of her sister could mean.

At length she said, "My sister, thy slave hath almost convinced me of the truth and power of this religion that she and our Julia have learned. At my desire she told me much concerning it on our voyage from Rome, but I needed something to convince me of its reality; although our Julia's braving the terrible pestilence was in itself a great puzzle, dreading, as we Romans do, going down into the dark world of shades. But to believe in a God who hath brought 'life and immortality to light' must take away this dread terror, and—"

But Valeria interposed with a passionate "Hush, hush! I cannot bear it; the shame and disgrace is too terrible. O, my father! my father! what wilt thou say when thou hearest that thy daughter Claudia, the pure and holy vestal, hath declared herself a Christian!" and, with a burst of anguish, Valeria hurried from the peristyle, and sought the secrecy of her own room to indulge her grief unmolested.

She drew the thick, embroidered curtain across the entrance that separated it from her bathroom, and, throwing herself on a couch, sobbed passionately for some time. By degrees, however, she became more calm, and when she heard Glaucia enter the outward room to prepare her bath she sat quite silent, so that the girl had no idea her mistress was so near. If she had she would scarcely have dared to do what she did. Having finished her preparations by pouring the perfume into the bath, placing the unguents and powders at hand, ready for her mistress's use, she kneeled down beside the bath, and, in the name of Christ, prayed that her mistress might bathe in the atoning blood that had been shed for her sins, that she might cast away the worship of the false gods, and trust only in the one true God who had made heaven and earth, and all the nations of men.

Valeria sat and listened to her slave in silent wonder. There was no petition for vengeance to fall upon her, no anger or hatred in the prayer, only she seemed to think she needed pardon for something, and she asked that pardon might be given.

When Glaucia had gone, Valeria left her room and went back to the peristyle, but found it deserted. Thinking that Julia and her sister had walked into the garden to talk over this new faith, she passed on to her father's chamber, to sit with him for a short time before taking her bath; but, to her surprise, Claudia was sitting with him reading one of the manuscripts of Epicurus. She looked up as Valeria entered and smiled gravely, but, at the same time, made a sign for her to be silent as to what had passed in the peristyle.

"My sister, I have taken your place, I fear," she said, rising as she spoke, and preparing to lay aside the manuscript.

The invalid sighed deeply as his eyes fell upon Valeria. "Claudia hath been reading to me on the old subject, but there is no light, Valeria; it is all dark, quite dark."

"What is quite dark, my father?" asked Valeria, thinking that his mind must be wandering.

"Every thing beyond the funeral urn. What the realm of shades may be—whether we are even shades—we cannot tell;" and the philosopher sighed wearily.

Claudia passed out of the room, and Valeria took up the manuscript, but her father motioned her to put it down.

"No more now," he said; "I shall know it all ere long. I must take this leap in the dark, as all my ancestors have done."

Valeria shivered. "My father, art thou worse to-day?" she asked.

"No, not worse, but no better. Have the sacrifices been sent to the temple of Jupiter?" he asked anxiously.

"Yes, my father, and I have myself been many times to the altar of Hygeia," said Valeria, "and yet thou dost not gain health."

"I would that I could gain the knowledge I have been seeking all my life," sighed the philosopher, "and which I thought I should be sure to gain here in Athens from the study of her various systems of philosophy. Valeria, it is to be found," he said with sudden energy, "and do thou seek it—search for it until thou find it, no matter in what direction the search may lead thee."

Suddenly there flashed upon Valeria's mind the words spoken by Julia in the peristyle a short time before, but she put them from her in angry scorn. "The God of those miserable Christians bring light and immortality to light when our noblest philosophers have failed! Impossible," muttered Valeria; and she went on carefully reading over the manuscript to herself, hoping to find some clew that would lead her to the light her father so earnestly longed for. But none could she find; it was, as her father said, dark, all dark, and, grope as she might, no ray of light came to reward her.

When she saw that her father was sleeping, she beckoned to the slave in the anteroom and bade her take her place, and then went to her bath. To her surprise, Claudia sat in her dressing-room, and asked her to dismiss Glaucia, as she wished to speak to her.

Valeria had not forgotten her sister's declaration of the morning, and was very cold and haughty in her manner.

"My sister, thou art thinking of my incautious words so imprudently spoken this morning," she said. "Forget them, I pray thee, as I shall strive to do; or, if that is impossible, try to think that I knew not what I said when they were spoken."

"Forget them," repeated Valeria, as if hardly comprehending her sister's meaning; "but, my sister, thou art—"

"I am Claudia the vestal still, and shall ever remain so," interrupted Claudia.

Valeria breathed a sigh of relief. "Sweet Flora be praised!" she uttered; "I was afraid thou wert about to act as rashly as Julia hath done."

Claudia shook her head, and turned her eyes to the ground. "There may be some truth in this new religion. I believe there is; but think of the disgrace I should incur if I publicly declared this, and openly joined this sect of people called Christians. Think of the scandal it would cause in Rome, the disgrace that would fall upon our family when the shameful tale was told that Claudia the vestal had forsaken the old gods of Rome and become a Christian."

Valeria kissed her sister in silent approval, and yet, while she did so, those haunting words of Julia's came back to her mind, "Life and immortality brought to light," linked this time with the charge her father had given her to continue her search for this truth in whatsoever direction it might be found. But again she argued that Julia's vaunting assertion could not be true, or her sister would not so lightly give up what she already knew, and, with this thought, she summoned Glaucia once more, and commenced her preparations for the bath.

How she should punish her waiting-maid for

daring to neglect the worship of the gods she did not know. To recall Fulvia and send Glaucia back among the household slaves did not suit her personal convenience, for, in spite of her presumption, she liked Glaucia; besides, no one could arrange her hair or dress her to her father's taste but the Greek girl. She did not, however, speak to her while she was at her bath, or while she was dressing her afterward—a fact that Glaucia noticed, and she wondered what her punishment would be. But her mistress was dressed, and she was left to clear up the dressing-room, and no word had been spoken beyond a haughty command to go to the market for some flowers when her present task was completed.

Glaucia's color went and came, and her heart beat with a feeling of almost tumultuous joy at the thought of seeing her friend once more, and she forgot every thing else for the time. Just as she was starting for the market, however, she was vexed to see Julia's maid, the little blind Jewess, coming toward her.

"What can she want now!" exclaimed Glaucia petulantly, as Drusilla said in a plaintive tone, "Is Glaucia near?"

"Yes," answered Glaucia shortly, "but I am going out."

"My mistress told me thou wert going to the

market, and desired me to ask thee if I might go also," said Drusilla.

Glaucia would have said "No," had she dared, but as it was she only yielded a reluctant consent, and they set off together hand in hand, neither speaking until the market-place was reached, when Glaucia looked eagerly round for her friend, who so often stood preaching at the entrance, and she could not help heaving a sigh of disappointment when she saw the empty space where a crowd had so often stood before. The cause of this, however, they overheard from the gossip of two market-women.

"The Nazarene will not come to-day, by Ceres," said one.

"The gods forbid that he should, until my pomegranates are sold, for these fierce Jews are watching for him, and there would be another riot," said her neighbor.

Drusilla raised her head quickly. "Who is this Nazarene?" she asked. "Is he called Paul?"

"Hush! hush!" said Glaucia. "Let them not hear thee talk of Paul, or they will know I used to linger here to listen to the words of one who learned the truth from his lips."

"The truth!" repeated Drusilla. "Dost thou believe that Paul preached the truth?"

Glaucia looked into the sightless eyes of her companion, as if asking whether she dare trust her secret to her, and then she whispered, "I am a Christian."

For answer, Drusilla threw her arms round her fellow-slave's neck, and, kissing her, said, "We are sisters then—sisters in Christ, who hath made all men one in himself."

Before Glaucia could recover from her astonishment at this avowal, her arm was seized by the blind girl just as a piercing scream was heard, and she said hastily,

"Glaucia, I know that voice—that scream. Lead me to him, for he is my friend, and I may be able to help him, as he once helped me."

CHAPTER XIII.

LAON'S SEARCH.

WHEN Laon landed in Athens, his first care was to hasten to the city and inquire for a noble Roman family who had lately come to reside there; but to all his inquiries men only shrugged their shoulders and told him so many noble Romans were coming and going now that it would not be easy to find the family he wanted, unless he knew what quarter they were living in; and advised him to commence his search at the fashionable end of the city.

This advice he decided to follow, as being the best course he could think of; and having received a few sesterces as wages from the shipmaster, he left the market-place and went on to the other end of the city and commenced his inquiries, resolving not to do any thing else until Glaucia was found. But, to his disappointment, no one had heard of the name of Gracchi here; and although he went on from one mansion to another, until he had to give up the search from weariness, he seemed no nearer the desired end than when he landed.

In a few days his small stock of money was spent, and then he resolved to go to some former friends of his father's and ask their help and advice in his difficulty. Laon was tired and hungry before he could decide to take this step, for he had long since thought that some of his father's friends might and ought to have come forward to save Glaucia at least from a life of slavery, and as they had not done so of their own free-will he would never ask help from them. This resolution, so easy to keep when at a distance, and while he felt sure of being able to find h's sister, had been gradually breaking down since the conviction had grown upon him that he should never succeed in his search by his own unaided efforts; and so, at last, he stood at the door of a wealthy old man who had known his family for many years, and who had often shown him little acts of kindness during his father's lifetime.

"Wilt thou tell thy master that Laon, the Athenian, craves an audience?" he said, with something of the assumption of manhood, to the slave who sat in the doorway and acted as porter.

Laon was careful to make the customary revcrence to the household gods as he crossed the threshold; but the man eyed him suspiciously, for his dress was not in accordance with the rank of his master's usual guests, and he told him to stand aside for a client to pass through the vestibule.

The blood rose to Laon's cheek as this request was enforced by a rude push, and he said hastily,

"Slave, dost thou dare to touch a Greek and an Athenian? I—"

"I have no time to talk to boys," said the slave sneeringly; "if thou desirest to see the noble Agamos thou must wait thy turn, like the rest;" and the man took his seat by the door again to question each new-comer before he passed into the vestibule.

Laon inwardly chafed at this treatment, but he was obliged to submit, and so passed into the vestibule, which was already nearly full of waiting clients.

"Agamos is a genuine lover of fine jewels," said one who carried a small casket, which he was careful not to trust out of his hand.

"Jewels I know nothing of, but if he is a judge of the true old Falernian he will buy what I come to offer him," said a wine merchant, whose rubicund face bespoke his own love of the rich old wine. "It is a chance not to be met with twice in a man's lifetime, I can tell thee, and Agamos must not miss it."

"Or thou wilt miss making a good bargain," laughed the jeweler.

"Well, it may be so," said his companion.

"But what have we here?" he added, as another came pressing in with several rich robes and tunics hanging over his arm.

"These are all in the newest style," said the fresh comer. "I have but just made them up from patterns received from Rome. This purple silk, edged with silver fringe, is exactly like one worn by the emperor the last time he played upon the lute before his people.

"It is very handsome, and well became Nero, I doubt not, for his long, fair curls would contrast with that rich purple," said the jeweler in a tone of admiration.

"Nero's taste is exquisite, from the color of a robe to a fight in the arena," said the man milliner; "and if I can only get our noble patron, Agamos, to think so, he will add a few of these to his wardrobe, and I shall be some sestercia the richer."

The others laughed. "And thou wilt persuade him that his iron-gray locks will rival the golden curls of Nero," said the jeweler.

"Well, and thou wilt do the same—wilt tell the poor, withered old man that thy finery will make him look as fresh and blooming as Poppea herself," retorted the man of cloth.

"Hold, there! Nothing but wine can warm the blood, and make us feel young again," said the wine merchant. "And since it is needful for our patron to feel young before he can look so, why I had better go in first, as you gentlemen will have a better chance of disposing of your finery after he has tasted my wine."

"Thou art a cunning fellow," said the jeweler; "but since I have little business on hand this morning thou mayest take my turn, and thou canst tell me then whether the umbra of Agamos is with him this morning."

"That is well spoken, my friend; and if I had a skin of this same Falernian to spare it should be at thy service; though I hope this umbra is not with our patron to-day, for he always protests that things can be bought cheaper in the market than honest men can afford to sell them in this part of Athens, so that it is hard to drive a bargain when he is at hand."

"Thou art of my own mind," said the habit-maker, "and yet I have sold this same fellow a tunic for less than the silk cost me that he might help me to make a good bargain with our patron. Ah! times are not as they used to be when I was a boy, like this one here;" and as he spoke he looked toward Laon, who had been pushed and hustled into a corner.

Several others glanced toward him now, and then there followed some mysterious nods and shakes of the head between whispered communications that passed from one to the other.

All Laon could hear was, "Very strange," "Quite disgraceful," "Never been heard of since;" but he knew from the glances directed toward him that he was in some way connected with this "strange," "disgraceful" subject, whatever it might be. He resolved, therefore, to speak to the wine merchant, as he appeared to be so well acquainted with him, and so, pushing his way nearer the front, he said,

"Thou knowest me, I believe; thou hast sold many skins of wine to my father, I think."

But the man shook his head. "Thou art quite mistaken," he answered quickly, looking at Laon as though he had never seen him before; "I have lived in Athens many years now, and I never serve any but the noblest citizens, so that I should not be likely to know thy father."

The hot blood rushed to Laon's face at this gratuitous insult, but he had begun to school his heart to bear indignities in silence, if not in patience, and he turned away without replying.

In a few minutes the slave posted at the door of the atrium drew aside the curtain, and motioned to the first of the crowd to go in. The next minute the umbra, or representative of the great man, put his head outside to see how many were waiting for an audience.

"My patron, the noble Agamos, will not be able to see ye all to-day," he said, frowning at the jeweler as he pressed forward.

Laon pushed his way to the front, too. "I must see him to-day," he said earnestly.

The umbra looked at him. "If thou art insolent, boy, thou shalt not see him to-day, or to-morrow either," he said.

"Wilt thou tell him that Laon, the son of a very old friend, wishes to see him?" said the boy, taking no notice of this speech.

"Laon, Laon," repeated the umbra. "O, I remember now," he suddenly added with a grim smile, "and, doubtless, my patron will remember thee likewise."

"Yes, my father was an Epicurean as well as Agamos," said Laon with a touch of pride in his tone.

A meaning smile passed over the faces of several, and again there was that mysterious whispering, which went on until the wine merchant passed on into the atrium. Laon was disappointed that he had not been summoned to go in before these clients and the different people that were waiting about, but he consoled himself with the thought that the man had forced his way in, and that he should be the next summoned. But he was not. Another and another went in, until at last, feeling sure that the umbra had forgotten he was there, he persuaded the slave in attendance—whose duty it was to lift the curtain on one side for each to pass in and out—to go and tell him that Laon was waiting.

"Laon may wait," was the message brought back, and not too civilly delivered: so he sat down with what patience he could muster, and saw one after another pass in and out again, until at last all had had an audience. Then he was allowed to enter; but the face of the old man grew dark as he entered his presence.

"Insolent, presumptuous boy, how dost thou dare obtrude thyself upon my notice!" he said.

Laon looked at him in silent wonder. "I

know not—I cannot tell," he stammered. "My father was thy friend, and—and—"

"And the greatest rogue in Athens, not to speak of thy mother and her disgrace," interrupted the old man angrily.

"My mother!" repeated Laon, and his face grew pale as he spoke. "Canst thou tell me what she did?"

"She was a woman," said the old man fiercely.

"Ah! that she was," assented the umbra.

"But what crime did she commit?" asked the boy.

"I tell thee she was a woman, and no better than the rest of her sex from Venus downward; nay, she was a great deal worse than other women," went on Agamos.

"Yes, much worse," corroborated the umbra.

"Well, since thou knowest so much about my mother, perhaps thou wilt tell me what it is she is accused of?" said Laon, turning to the humble companion of the great man.

He looked at his patron, and lifted his hands deprecatingly, but did not utter a word. It was not his duty to say a word on his own account, but merely to reiterate what his master said.

"Thou art insolent, boy!" said Agamos; "wherefore hast thou forced thyself into our presence."

"I came to ask thy help as the friend of my dead father," said Laon; "but, since all friendship seems to be forgotten, I will not press my suit further."

"Nay, I am not likely to forget a friendship that cost me so dear," said Agamos. "Thy father borrowed too many of my sestercia for me to forget him quickly," he added.

"Yes, that he did," responded the umbra.

"I am sorry," said Laon, and in this he spoke truly. "And since my father borrowed so much, I will not seek to add to the debt by asking thee to give to his son either money or advice;" saying which Laon bowed, and hurried from the atrium as quickly as his tottering limbs would carry him.

He was faint with hunger before he came, and now, after these hours of waiting, he could hardly stand. As he walked through the vestibule one of the slaves passed him with a basket of figs and pomegranates, and he felt strongly inclined to take some; but he resisted the temptation, and walked out into the street feeling hopeless as well as hungry.

Which way he should turn or what he should do now he did not know, and the thought of Glaucia and her possible danger if she offended her mistress made him groan aloud in agony of spirit. Then there was his mother and the dark mystery that seemed to enfold her. What had she done? Why had his father married again? Where was she at this time? To all these questions Laon longed to find an answer; but how he was to set about it, what the first step even ought to be, he was puzzled to know, and what hope would he have to commence such a search when he could not find Glaucia, although he knew she was in Athens.

There was one question, however, that would have to be answered before any of these—one want that was clamoring to be satisfied, and now, even before Glaucia could be searched for again, he must have some food. He had thought to obtain this from Agamos, but as he had given him insults instead of help and advice, he resolved to seek another of his father's friends.

He had to walk some distance before the house was reached, for he was by no means so wealthy as Agamos, and did not live in the fashionable part of Athens. Two or three slaves formed the whole household here, and there was no crowd of clients waiting for an audience, and Laon hoped that this follower of Epicurus would receive him more favorably than the last.

There was little difficulty in gaining an

entrance, and Laon was shown into the atrium, where the would-be philosopher was reclining on a couch, with a silver cup by his side containing sweet wine. His brows were crowned with a garland, and a soft perfume filled the air; and as he rose languidly to gaze at Laon his loose flowing robe disclosed an embroidered tunic, such as Valeria might have worn.

"I do not remember thee," he said lazily, as Laon mentioned his name.

"Nay, but thou knewest my father before he passed to the realm of shades," said Laon.

The man lifted his hand as if to screen his eyes from viewing some dreadful specter.

"Nay, nay, talk not of such dull subjects to a follower of Epicurus; let us eat and drink while we can without troubling ourselves any further. Life was given that we might enjoy it, and I mean to do so, too," he said, taking a draught of wine as he spoke.

Laon looked perplexed. "Thou wert a friend of my father's," he said, "and I have come to ask thee—" and there Laon hesitated.

"Go on," said the man, "perhaps I can help thee. I doubt not thou hast come to ask me to supper, but scarcely knowest how to frame the invitation. Make thyself easy, I am not one of those who carp at the exact words an invitation is given in when the supper is good."

Laon's face grew crimson. "I have no supper for myself," he said, speaking with a desperate effort; "indeed, it was that I might get one I have come to thee now."

The languid-looking exquisite stared at him in blank amazement. "Thou hast come to ask a poor man like me to give thee a supper when I can scarcely get one for myself? It is an insult—an outrage! begone from my presence, or my slave shall kick thee out:" and he seemed so overcome by this display of energy that he fell back on the couch as if quite exhausted.

Laon went out into the street, and, hungry as he was, he felt he would rather starve than attempt begging of friends again. He would look for some work now, and earn a few sesterces, and go on with his search for Glaucia in the best way he could, without asking any body's advice or help either

CHAPTER XIV.

FRIENDS IN NEED.

HOW to earn a few sesterces was a question more easily asked than answered, and Laon found himself wandering up and down the streets of Athens hungry and tired, without home and without friends, not knowing where to obtain even a meal.

Wandering on toward the Marathon gate he overtook a man slowly laboring along under a load of empty baskets, honey jars, and snow pitchers, cursing his ill luck, and calling upon all the gods in turn to help him. The only response he obtained to these objurgations was the laughter and jeers of the passers-by with an occasional shower of stones from the boys, until Laon overtook him. He might have joined the ranks of his tormentors at another time, but his own helpless, friendless condition made him pity the poor man, although he could not help smiling at his ludicrous efforts to get along quicker with his load, and evade the stones that were thrown at him

At length Laon stepped up to the old man and said, "I will carry one or two of thy baskets for thee."

The man looked at him suspiciously and shook his head. "If I were only Jupiter," he said, "I would give ye boys something to do."

"Well, I want to do something," said Laon. "I want to earn some money, but I am willing to help thee with the baskets for nothing."

"Nay, if thou wilt help me carry some of these jars and baskets home I will give thee a few sesterces and as many ripe figs as thou canst eat," said the man.

"I will carry them," said Laon; and in a few minutes he had taken his share of the load, and was trudging on at the man's side, listening to his account of how his mule had fallen lame, and the straps of the pannier had broken that morning just as he got to the market.

They took the road leading to Corinth after passing through the city gate, and Laon was not sorry when they stopped, about a mile beyond, and the old man announced that they had reached home. The poor boy was so exhausted with his long walk and the almost superhuman efforts he had made to keep up, that when he put the jars and baskets down upon the ground he sunk down beside them.

"Why! thou art looking ill, boy," said the old man; "rest here awhile and I will fetch thee a little wine and honeycomb;" and he threw down his own load and passed into the farm-house close by.

In a minute or two a stout, rosy-looking matron came out, bringing a cup of wine and a few figs, but when she saw Laon she set down the cup, and, kneeling by his side, exclaimed—

"Laon, my boy, my own nursling! why, what ails thee; what hath brought thee back from thy rich kinsman in Rome?"

The sound of the well-known kindly voice of his nurse recalled Laon's fleeting senses, and he slowly opened his eyes and looked in her face, and then at the jars and baskets by his side.

"Am I dreaming, or is it really Lepida," he said faintly, passing his hand before his eyes and looking up into her face.

She stooped and kissed him. "Nay, nay, be sure it is thy nurse, Lepida, herself," she said kindly.

Laon nestled against the supporting arm. "O Lepida, I am so hungry!" he said.

"Hungry!" she repeated, as though she could not understand such a thing in connection with Laon. "Ah! ah!" she said, "thou hast often been hungry before when we have been to the market and thou sawest my good man's pomegranates. I could not give them to thee then," she added, "but thou shalt have as many as thou wilt now."

"Nay, I would rather have a little millet or barley-cake," said Laon, "for I am so hungry I know not what to do."

The poor woman's eyes filled with tears, but she did not waste any time in useless words or grief now. She got him to drink the wine, and then half led, half carried him into the house, smiling through her tears at his look of wondering perplexity.

"It is my house, my home," she said; "Arnobius asked me to be his wife, and help him keep his bees last moon, and so we were married, and I left the city and came here;" and she looked round the roomy kitchen with evident pride and pleasure.

There was no need for an atrium in a house where the inhabitants spent a greater part of their time out of doors, and so this space was taken up by a large store-room and kitchen, all in one. Only the center of this was held sacred to the lares and penates, the same as with the ordinary atrium, and the images ot these household gods occupied the middle of the floor, and under them was spread a tiny square of costly carpet, woven in the looms of Sardis, and of which Lepida was not a little proud.

The rest of the floor or pavement was of clay, baked hard, and there was an exquisite statue of Ceres as well as of Pan, and a sacred tripod for their worship; while round the room were shelves, on which jars of honey stood ready to take to market. The pots, pans, and buckets, which were arranged on a lower shelf, were of bronze, and all of a most elegant and graceful shape, although for such homely uses.

Laon looked round the room and heaved a sigh of relief as he noticed these evidences of comfort and easy competence. "Lepida, thou wilt be able to give me a meal," he said in an eager whisper.

"Hush! hush! thou wilt break my heart, Laon," she said. "Yes, indeed, thou shalt have a meal as long as I have one to share with thee;" and she seated him on the rough couch, and proceeded to spread the evening repast at once.

In a few minutes her husband came into the room, and his wife explained who their visitor was.

"He is right welcome, my Lepida," said the

old man, "for there was not a boy in Athens who offered to help me with my baskets to-day save him only. Give him the best of our cheese and honeycomb, and the choicest morsels of the kid thou art stewing."

Lepida shook her finger at her husband playfully. "What right hast thou to go peeping into my stew-pans?" she said; "but hasten now and bring in the baskets," she added, "or Laon shall eat all the kid;" and she bustled out of the room to finish her preparations, giving Laon a few figs to eat while she prepared the supper and placed it on the table.

Every thing was plain and homely, but to Laon it was the richest feast he had known for a long time. The kid was delicious, and so was the parched corn and barley bread, and the cakes made of figs and nuts pressed hard. He ate slowly and cautiously, for he was almost starved, and Lepida, noticing this, gave him the most tender morsels, telling him at the same time not to hurry over his meal.

"My Arnobius must go and drive home the goats by and by, but I have little to do, and so I can sit by while thou art telling me all that has happened to thee and Glaucia," said Lepida when the meal was almost over, so far as she and her husband were concerned.

At the mention of Glaucia the tears slowly welled up into Laon's eyes as he said, "Alas! Lepida, I fear I shall never see her again!"

"Never see thy sister again!" repeated his nurse. "Nay, nay, if thou hast been rash in leaving thy wealthy kinsman he will not be so hard as to deny thee speech with Glaucia when thou shalt wish it, or he is—"

"Who told thee we were going to a wealthy kinsman?" interrupted Laon.

"Nemesa, thy step-mother, ere she left Athens with her son," replied Lepida.

"It was false, Lepida," said Laon fiercely, "we were sold—Glaucia and I—sold to pay our father's debts."

"Sold!" exclaimed Lepida, starting from her seat. "The children whom I took from their mother and promised to cherish as my own, sold!"

"Thou didst take care of us as long as thou wert able," said Laon, laying his hand tenderly on hers, and trying to soothe her agitation; "thou couldst not prevent us being taken to the slave-market by our father's creditor."

"And ye were both sold as slaves!" said Lepida, with a choking sob.

"No, I escaped—ran away from the market; but Glaucia was sold and brought back to

Athens, and when I found it out I came to look for her."

"My Glaucia is in Athens, then! The gods be praised for bringing her back to her friends! But why didst thou not bring her with thee?" she suddenly asked.

"I cannot find her," said Laon sadly; "she is waiting-maid to a noble Roman lady, but no one in Athens seems to have heard of the Gracchi, although I was assured they came to settle here."

"Well, if they are in Athens my Arnobius can find it out, for, I assure thee, he is the greatest gossip in the market. I doubt not the pannier-straps were cut while he was discussing the last bit of news from the Areopagus," she said with a pleasant smile.

"Then thou dost not go to the market, Lepida," said Laon.

"Nay, who would look after the house if I wasted my time at Athens?" she said. "But look not so anxious," she continued, "Arnobius will find our Glaucia."

"It was not alone of Glaucia I was thinking, but of my mother, too," said Laon with a deep-drawn sigh.

The woman looked anxious and troubled too, and shook her head sadly. "Thou hast forgotten the advice I gave thee with the parchments," she said. "I bid thee forget thou hadst ever had a mother."

"But I cannot forget it, Lepida," said Laon. "I am not a child now, and I mean to find my mother," he added in a tone of determination.

The woman started. "Hast thou read what is written on the parchment?" she asked anxiously.

"Alas! thou knowest I cannot read yet, but I mean to learn as speedily as may be," answered Laon; "for if this that my mother hath written is a secret, no one should know it save her son, therefore I have refrained from showing it to any stranger. Dost thou know what this writing is?" he suddenly asked.

The woman shook her head. "I have not even looked upon it," she said. "Thy mother, before she left Athens, bound me by a terrible oath to deliver the parchments to her children so soon as they should be grown up, and that no one should look upon them or touch them until they were delivered into thy hand."

"And thou hast kept thy promise faithfully. I thank thee, Lepida, for it may be that when I learn to read I shall be able to find my mother through this writing—she may even be in Athens now," he added.

"Nay, she may not come within the gates of our city," said the woman with a sigh.

"Then my mother was banished by the judges," said Laon quickly. "What was her crime?" he asked.

But Lepida could only shake her head. "The gods and men alike were offended," she said.

"I will know what her offense was," said Laon in a determined tone. "I have heard her spoken of this day as no Greek matron should be, and I *will* know what cause she hath given for it."

Lepida sighed, but did not reply, and shortly afterward her husband came in to ask some questions about the bee-hives. When these were answered, she asked him if he had heard any thing of a noble Roman family, named Gracchi, who had recently come to Athens.

The subject, however, was not a pleasant one to Arnobius. "Ask me not about these upstarts," he said, "or I'm afraid I shall lose my temper."

"Nay, nay, but I must find out where these Gracchi live, and thou must not lose thy temper," said his wife.

"I will have naught to do with Romans, not even to ask about them," said the old man. "If thou art so anxious about these vain coxcombs who come here and ape the manners of our Plato—as though that would give them his wisdom—let Laon come with me to the market, and he can ask in some of the booths; some of our gossips will have heard of them, I doubt not."

"That will I do most gladly," answered Laon, "and if I can help thee while we are there I will do it also."

"Laon, thou art a sensible lad," said the old man, "too sensible for the life of a city; thou couldst drive a bargain, I doubt not, and look after a market-stall too."

"Yes, I think I could," said Laon.

"Well, if thou art willing, thou shalt try; and if thou canst, and hast a mind to stay with us awhile, thou shalt be welcome to bed and board and a few sesterces besides. What sayest thou, Lepida," he asked, turning to his wife.

She hardly knew what to say. That Laon was pleased at the proposal and would be glad to accept it she could see, but it was such a reversion of all that she deemed right and proper—such a humble position for one born to expect such a different station in life—that she could only shake her head dubiously.

"I know what thou art thinking of, Lepida," said Laon; "but what am I to do if I take not this kind offer of thy husband. I have tried begging, and will never do that any more; and starving, and hope to have no more of that; I have no learning, therefore, there is nothing but work I can do."

"But thou, a noble-born Athenian, to be selling honey and grapes in the market!" objected Lepida.

"It is better to sell these than to be sold," said Laon. "And I have stood in the shambles with barbarian Britons."

"I could see to thy comforts here, and take care that thou hadst no menial work to do in the fields," debated Lepida.

"And I should have time to learn the art of reading and writing," said Laon. "Lepida, say thou wilt agree to this plan, for my sake," he urged.

She could not resist that pleading face and voice. "Well, thou shalt try it, my Laon," she said, "and I will be thy nurse still; only thou must not go to the market yet—not until thou art stronger and more fit for work than thou art now."

Laon objected to this delay at first, but was obliged to yield the point, for he felt himself more weak the next morning than he expected; so weak, indeed, that he could scarcely creep about the house and garden, and needed the kind offices of his nurse in more ways than one.

He grew more reconciled to this, however, when Lepida lent him a manuscript containing the first rudiments of reading. With this in his hand he went and sat under the shade of the mulberry-tree that sheltered one side of the house, and by close application had learned to spell out a few words before nightfall, for the first step had already been mastered—he knew the Greek alphabet—and so it would not be so difficult for him to learn to read.

CHAPTER XV.

TIDINGS.

LAON was glad to go to the market and commence his work, although it was some days before Lepida would allow him to do so. But he felt the wisdom of the restriction that had been imposed upon him before he reached the market, for he was so tired that he could scarcely stand when the fruit-stall was reached at which Arnobius set out his wares.

Pomegranates and grapes, figs and honey, were displayed in most tempting groups, and then Laon was left to serve the customers for a short time, while Arnobius went to another part of the market to make some purchases for his wife.

Laon was to carry these home to her at mid-day by himself if the fruit was not all sold by that time, so that they could return together, an arrangement that did not please Arnobius very well, as he wanted to leave his stall in charge of Laon while he went to listen to a learned disputation that was to take place between two philosophers, an Epicurean and a Stoic, on the immortality of the soul.

Lepida, however, must have her merchandise whatever her husband's intellectual wants might be, and so, as there had been but few customers during the morning, Laon was dispatched with the laden basket in good time, so that he might reach home before the sun attained its meridian height.

The basket being heavy, and Laon tired, he did not walk very fast until, drawing near the Marathon gate, he was overtaken by a cohort of Roman soldiers, when he resolved to keep up with these, both for company and protection, for robbery was not infrequent even in broad daylight, and within sight of the city gates.

Laon had to walk fast, however, to keep up with the Roman steeds, and he wondered several times why they were going at such a moderate pace. The reason, however, was explained just as he turned into the lane leading to his new home, for the soldiers suddenly halted, and, looking back, Laon saw another cavalcade aproaching, headed by lictors and an elegant chariot, so that he concluded at once that the second party were going to join the soldiers for safety.

He did not wait for them to come up, for he

knew Lepida would be wanting the contents of his basket, and so he hurried into the house just as Anicetus with his train passed. If he had only known Glaucia was in that company, or if she could have been told that the pretty, quaint, brown house she admired was the home of her old nurse, and the dwelling-place of her beloved brother, what a load would have been lifted from the heart of each.

But neither knew that the other was so near, and so Glaucia went on her way to Delphi, praying to her newly-found God to take care of her brother and bring them together once more; while Laon related to his friend and nurse how he had inquired of the market people for the family to whom his sister had been sold, but that no one had heard of the name of Gracchi.

"Then, perhaps, they did not come to Athens at all," said Lepida.

"Yes, I feel sure they did," answered Laon, "for the old slave who told me would not tell a lie. Yes, yes, they are here," he added confidently; "I will yet find Glaucia, and then—then—" and Laon stopped.

"What wouldst thou say?" asked Lepida.

"I have determined to free Glaucia," said Laon, breathing hard, "and I have heard news in the market this morning which, if true, will enable me to do so, I think."

"Why, what hast thou heard? Is Plutus going to send showers of sesterces upon Athens?" asked Lepida with a smile.

"Not exactly, but something like it," said Laon. "The Roman cohort bringing letters from Rome to our prefect hath likewise brought the news that the great Emperor Nero purposes to visit Athens next spring. He is coming to witness the Isthmian games at Corinth, and will bring with him his favorite gladiators to instruct some Greek lads in the use of the cestus."

Lepida looked scornfully. "We have altars to Astrea and Ate; but we have not yet thrown down the altar of mercy," she said.

Laon looked as though he did not comprehend what she meant. "The emperor will not throw down the altars of our gods; all worships are permitted at Rome," he said.

"Yes, and so are all cruelties, or there would be no gladiators—not even the poorest of our Theti will patronize these," said Lepida, speaking quickly.

Laon looked down. "These gladiators are brave men," he said, "or they would not be so careless of death."

"It is the bravery of brute beasts, then, not of wise men," said Lepida. "Think of our heroes who fought at Marathon; they were brave, for they died that Athens might be free; but these men dare death for the sake of a few sestercia."

"But suppose they fought that somebody they loved might be free," said Laon in a lower tone, "would they not be brave then?" he asked.

Lepida started and gazed into the boyish face looking so earnest and so determined, and in that moment she comprehended what he intended. Seizing his arm, she said, "Laon, thou must not do this."

A faint color stole into his cheeks. "I *must* free Glaucia," he said.

"But not in this way. The gods forbid that thou shouldst become a gladiator!" she exclaimed impulsively.

"But it is the only way I can ever hope to earn money enough to ransom my sister," he said with a sigh.

"And suppose thou failest?" she asked. "Suppose thou art the conquered instead of the conqueror, and needest the death penny put into thy mouth instead of receiving the sestercia in thy hand."

"But I must not, will not, fail," said Laon; "the gods will help me. I will sacrifice to Fortunatus each time I pass through the city."

Lepida wrung her hands in anguish. "Laon, thou knowest not what thou art saying. Thou knowest not what the life of a gladiator is."

"Indeed I do. The gladiators were kind to me in Rome, and offered to get me admittance to their famous school; and if Appius comes with the emperor he will teach me how to use the cestus and net, and trident, too, I doubt not," said Laon, not in the least moved by his nurse's aversion to the games.

Lepida grew pale, and her hands worked convulsively; but at last she said, "Laon, for thy mother's sake thou must not do this."

"For my mother's sake!" repeated Laon; "but what would my mother say if she knew Glaucia was a slave and I did not try to free her?"

"Thou shalt try," said Lepida eagerly; "thou shalt do any thing thou wilt to ransom her—any thing but become a gladiator," she added, repressing a shudder.

"But why would my mother object to my becoming a gladiator?" asked Laon pettishly.

"Canst thou, being a Greek—an Athenian—ask such a question?" said Lepida evasively.

"It is considered a brave and noble profession in Rome," grumbled Laon; "and if thou canst not tell me why my mother would object to it, I do not see why I should not practice it."

Lepida could not stay to talk to him any longer, and so he was left to vent his ill humor alone, while she went about her daily work.

The next day Laon renewed his inquiries among the people he saw in the market, and at last met with a slave who could tell him where Fabrizzio Gracchi lived.

To leave the stall and go at once in search of Glaucia again was the work of a few minutes; but when at last the house was reached, the slave sitting at the door told him the family were away, and most of the slaves were with them.

"But, perhaps, there is one left behind. I want my sister, a Greek girl called Glaucia. Do you know where she is?"

"Glaucia is on her way to Delphi with the noble Valeria, her mistress," said the slave.

"When will she return?" asked Laon, scarcely able to restrain his tears.

"That were a puzzle to tell any one; she went but yesterday, and, as thou knowest, the journey is a dangerous one."

The old man seemed inclined to gossip, but Laon was in no mood for this, and turned sorrowfully away and went back to the market, resolving to call at the mansion every day until his sister returned, for fear she should come back and set off on another journey at once, since it seemed these Romans were so fond of traveling.

Lepida tried to dissuade him from adopting this plan, saying the slave would grow weary of answering his inquiry so often; but Laon was willful and headstrong, as lads of his age frequently are, and, as Lepida had foreseen, he was told at last that if he came there again he should be kicked down the steps, and so he could only go and look at the house and wonder when Glaucia would be back, whether she had already arrived, and why she did not come out sometimes as well as the other slaves.

He ventured to ask one of these for her again after some little time, and then he heard that she was ill and had been left behind at Corinth, and he hurried home at once to inform Lepida of it.

"At Corinth," repeated the woman, turning pale, "why did they take her to Corinth?"

"Nay, I cannot tell; but I am going to search for her now," said Laon.

But Lepida laid her hand upon his shoulder,

"Laon," she said, "thou must not go to Corinth."

"Why not?" he asked. "I am not a child now; I can—"

"Dost thou remember what thou saidst the other day about wishing thou hadst taken my advice?" interrupted his nurse.

"Yes; it would have been better then, but now I must—"

"Thou must follow my advice now, Laon," said the woman sadly. "I will go to Corinth myself and search for Glaucia, and, if possible, bring her back with me."

"Thou go to Corinth, Lepida!" said Laon, opening his eyes in astonishment.

"Yes; I have been there many times," said the woman quietly. "I have other business that will take me there now besides searching for Glaucia," she added.

"Then let me go with thee and search for my sister while thou art about thy other business," said Laon.

But Lepida shook her head. "Nay, nay," she said; "thou must stay and take care of he house and Arnobius, for I have not been to Corinth since my marriage, and, doubtless, my husband will miss me, but if he has thee with him it will not be so bad."

"I had better go to Corinth with thee, I am sure," he said in a discontented tone.

Lepida, however, was firm. She would start on her journey at day-break the next morning and return in a few days, as soon as she had found Glaucia.

"But how art thou going to bring her back with thee?" asked Laon; "she is a slave and ill."

"True, she is a slave, but her mistress may be willing to sell her if I can only get sesterces enough," said Lepida; but how she was going to obtain the money, or whom she was going to see in the city, she would not say, and Laon was obliged to see her depart the next morning with her basket of dried dates and leather bottle of sweet wine, without having either his anxiety or curiosity satisfied.

Arnobius had fretted and grumbled a good deal at first over his wife's journey, but he assented at last, although he declared he could not spare Laon from the market now, and, therefore, the house would have to take care of itself while she was away. The fact was, Laon was left to take care of the stall a good deal now, for his master went off to another part of the market every day about the same hour, and when he came back he seemed too preoccupied to know what pricc to ask for his honcy or grapes.

Knowing the old man's love of gossip, Laon did not notice this much at first; but the day after Lepida went to Corinth, having sold out his things earlier than usual, he resolved to walk round the market-place and see what it was that interested Arnobius so much. He went to where the philosophers usually held their debates, but the space was deserted to-day, and, looking toward the entrance, he thought they must have chosen another spot for their disputations, for a dense crowd was standing round a venerable-looking man who seemed to be haranguing them from an elevated stone in the center. He crossed over the intervening space at once and eagerly pushed his way to the front, for the double purpose of seeing whether Arnobius was there and likewise hearing what was said.

"Jupiter, Apollo, Diana, and Pallas Athene, with every lesser god and goddess, are but vain idols, insulting to the one true God, who created all things and all men," said the old man boldly as Laon made his appearance in the very front rank of the crowd.

He looked up half expecting to see the statue of their renowned goddess descend from its pedestal and strike the offender dead, and some such feeling seemed to go through the crowd, of which fact the old man at once took advantage.

"Men and brethren, I affirm that the goddess is an idol, dumb and helpless as the stone upon which I am standing, and if I lie, let her now come down from yonder pedestal and defend her own honor."

A stillness like that of death held the crowd for a minute or two after these daring words were uttered, and then there arose a murmur of men's voices.

"He is an atheist and blasphemer," said some.

"Nay, nay, but the old man is right, Nazarene though he be. Let Pallas Athene come down and show us some of her mighty works if she be indeed a goddess," said a voice that was raised above all the rest. Laon recognized it in a moment, for it was Arnobius who spoke.

"Well said, old fruit-seller!" responded one; "if this 'Unknown God' has revealed himself of late let us hear all about him. Go on with thy reasoning, we would hear more of this resurrection thou wert speaking of," he added, turning to the preacher.

He was willing enough to continue his sermon, and Laon stood and listened until the close, and the truths that he taught he recognized as being the same for which Paul was now in prison, and which the sailor-Christian had taught his comrades on their voyage from Rome.

Arnobius looked somewhat confused when he saw Laon, and on their way home he said, "Tell not Lepida I have been listening to the old Nazarene preacher, for she hateth this new sect very sorely I know."

"Does she," said Laon carelessly. "Well, I think they speak truly, for I heard of wonderful miracles performed by this 'Unknown God' through the prayer of the prisoner Paul," and he went on to tell of his visit to him, and likewise of the brave, bold sailor who had been with him when he was shipwrecked.

"Well, I have begun to doubt the power of the gods lately," said Arnobius, "and I should like to put them to the test, if I could."

"Well, suppose, instead of pouring out a libation to them this evening, we spit on them and turn their faces to the wall. If they are gods and not idols they will surely turn round again," said Laon quickly.

Such a proposal shocked the old man at first,

but at length he consented to adopt it as a test while Lepida was out of the way. It was with a trembling hand, however, that he turned his marble deities to the wall. That, with the omission of the customary acts of worship, would be insulting enough, he thought, without the other addition, and he wondered whether Pomona would destroy all his fruit, Pan all his bees, and Ceres blight his fields while he was sleeping.

CHAPTER XVI.

THE RIOT.

WITH the first dawning rays of light Arnobius was up, anxiously examining the rows of bee-hives that stood along the side of the house, and he breathed a sigh of relief to find that they were all safe. In the darkness and stillness of the night he had half repented the dishonor he had shown to his gods, but, finding that every thing was safe, his courage rose again, and, as he prepared to set off to the market, he resolved to seek a private audience with the Nazarene, to ask him some questions about the great God whose message he proclaimed.

Pan, Ceres, and Pomona, his favorite deities, were still left with their faces to the wall when he went to the market, and he was more thoughtful and less talkative on his way there, a fact Laon noticed, although his own thoughts were occupied upon Lepida and her journey, wondering when she would be back and whether she would bring his sister with her.

The stall was set out, and the mule was tethered, and scarcely a word was spoken by either of them until the Christian preacher passed on his way to his customary stand near the entrance. He exchanged a few words with Arnobius as he passed, for he had learned to know him as one of his most constant and attentive hearers.

Soon after he had passed a party of Jews came along, looking fierce and angry, and watching them round the market. Arnobius saw that every empty space was occupied by others of the same nation.

"Laon, these proud, stiffnecked Jews mean mischief I can see," said the old man; "thou shalt guard the stall awhile, and if need be pack up the things, but go not from the market until I come back."

"Where art thou going?" asked Laon, growing somewhat pale as he noticed the gathering crowd of Jews. "Will there be a tumult, thinkest thou?" for he had heard of several riots in the agora.

"I know not, but I fear some evil is intended to the old Nazarene, and if there is, I will be at hand to strike a blow for him, since he will not strike for himself," said Arnobius.

"But the pomegranates and melons," said

Laon; "suppose the crowd should rush upon the stall."

"If thou canst save them do so, but I, at least, must defend the brave old Christian; his life is worth more than a few baskets of fruit and jars of honey;" saying which Arnobius hurried away, leaving Laon in a maze of doubt as to the sanity of his master.

What would careful, thrifty Lepida say if she knew that things were left to take care of themselves, while her husband went to take up the quarrel of the leader of this despised sect of Nazarenes?

As the Jews entered the market in large numbers at every avenue all the peace-loving customers retired, and very soon all business was suspended.

Laon was not long putting away his stores in a place of safety, and then he went to see what was going on near the entrance. He could see nothing but a swaying crowd of angry people, Jews and booth-keepers, with a few slaves, and one or two of the more respectable citizens; but it was easy to distinguish from the fierce, denunciatory words of the Jews that they were trying to rouse the anger of these against the Nazarenes as a sect, and the old preacher in particular.

Loud words, violent gesticulations, and threatening attitudes, with frequent appeals to the statue of the popular goddess in the center of the market, was all that could be heard, until at length a young man, more brave than prudent, cried, "Shame upon the Jews, ye are traitors and cowards!" and, in order to reach the front rank, he fought his way forward with blows.

This was the signal for other blows to be struck, and soon the market resounded with shrieks and curses, and cries of "Down with the Nazarenes! down with the atheists!" while blows fell thick and fast, stalls were thrown down, and the boards taken used as missiles. These, used almost aimlessly and in blind fury, struck down friend and foe, and the groans and screams of those knocked down and being trampled upon were heard on every side.

At first Laon tried to reach his master, whom he felt sure was near the Christian preacher; but he soon saw how hopeless this attempt was likely to be, and so kept at a safe distance from the scene of horror and confusion. Now and then he was called upon to render some assistance as one after another was dragged out of the terrible fray bleeding, wounded, insensible, almost dying.

The struggle grew fiercer as time went on, and

Laon sickened at the horrible spectacle, for now that the crowd had tasted blood, like the tiger it seemed to thirst for more, and all attempts to quell the fray were useless.

At last a cohort of Roman soldiers marched upon the scene of action, and the rioters were threatened with the points of their spears; while a few, who obstinately refused to cease fighting, were arrested and sent off to the prefect.

By this means quiet was at length restored, and Laon ventured once more in search of his master, though how he might find him, whether wounded or even dead, he could not tell. He might be among the prisoners; for if he had escaped both these fates why did he not come back, as he had promised.

Laon asked himself this question again and again as the market was slowly cleared of the combatants, and nothing remained to testify of the fight but a few blood-stained rags torn from the backs, of Jews or Athenians, some broken boards, and shattered stalls. Thinking at last that he had better take his fruit and honey out of the booth, where he had placed them for safety, and go home, he went in search of the mule, but, to his alarm, found that some one had untethered it, and, leaving the empty panniers in its place, had taken it for his own use.

The fruit and honey, therefore, had to be left in the booth, and Laon turned his steps homeward, while a dread feeling began to take possession of his mind that all this had happened through the anger of the gods whom he and Arnobius had insulted. He had always been taught that they were cruel and vengeful in their anger, and perhaps this was but a beginning of the calamities that were to follow upon the daring insult offered them the previous evening. They might even visit his offense upon his innocent sister, and the thought of this made him resolve to appease them if he could as soon as he reached home.

But other work awaited his arrival at the farm-house. Before he reached the door he saw the mule quietly grazing beside the myrtle hedge, so he knew that his master must have reached home, and he hurried in to ask him how he had escaped. But, to his surprise, the old Christian teacher, instead of Arnobius, was sitting in the kitchen. He was very pale, and bleeding from a deep cut on his shoulder, from which every vestige of clothing was torn; but he smiled as Laon entered—such a sweet, grave, peaceful smile it was, that, coming after Laon's troubled, anxious thoughts about the anger of his gods, seemed to give assurance of rest, peace, and confidence in his God, such as few enjoyed.

Arnobius came in just after Laon entered, looking anxious and troubled. "I know not what to do, Laon," he said. "He is sore wounded, as thou seest, and yet he insists upon returning to Athens to-night."

"My God will defend me," said the Christian calmly.

"If they were men and not wild beasts thy words would prevail with them, and there would be no need of blows," said Arnobius fiercely, "but since they—"

"Nay, nay, my brother, God will defend his own," said the Christian; "and the Lord Christ, whom I serve, hath given commandment that if thine enemy smite thee on one cheek thou shalt turn to him the other also."

"And they would strike that even as they did this day, and not only thy cheek but thy shoulder also; and as for talk about giving thy coat, they have taken all thy garments or torn them;" and Arnobius proceeded to wash the bruised and bleeding shoulder, and then bind it up after pouring in some choice olive oil that was kept only for the service of the gods.

The old man smiled at seeing the sacred oil used for his wound, and he glanced at the statues with their faces turned to the wall. "My brother, thou art casting off the old idolatry, but art thou seeking the one God, who can alone take the place of these in thy heart?"

"Ah, my father, I have long been seeking this 'Unknown God,' but I have found him at last," said Arnobius in a serious tone.

The Christian grasped his hand. "The Lord be thanked and praised!" he said in a triumphant tone; "what are wounds and bruises beside such joy as this, to know that another hath embraced this offer of mercy sent from our God."

"I would that thou couldst tarry and teach me somewhat more of the truths of this new faith. I am ignorant, as thou knowest, and all that I can tell thee is, that my heart has been taken captive by thy God, and I would that I could live or die to serve him, if such poor service as mine can be accepted by one so great and holy."

Laon was startled to hear Arnobius say these words in such a tone of earnestness that no one could doubt their sincerity; but he joined in begging the old man to stay, saying that he had a certain parchment that he greatly desired him to read.

Laon had managed to master the art of reading sufficiently to know something of the import of the words written on the parchment given him by Lepida, but he was anxious to know fully what this message of his mother's could be, for it might help him to understand what her offense had been.

The prayer of two anxious to be instructed in the Divine life could not be resisted, and, upon Arnobius promising that he should depart the next morning in time to appear before the judgment-seat of the prefect to plead on behalf of the prisoners, the old man agreed to stay, and when the evening meal was over Laon brought out his precious roll of parchment, that he might know the all-important message it contained. He was careful, however, not to mention his mother's name in connection with it.

"Lepida had given it to him for a keepsake before he went to Rome," he said, when asked how it came into his possession.

Slowly the little roll was unwound, but a look of joyful surprise beamed in his face as he looked over the neatly written lines. It was headed

"Good News from the 'Unknown God:' 'I will be a Father unto you, and ye shall be my sons and daughters, saith the Lord Almighty....

who hath reconciled us to himself by Jesus Christ, for God was in Christ reconciling the world unto himself, not imputing their trespasses unto them. Be ye reconciled to God.' "

"It is good news," said the old man, slowly and fervently, as he laid down the parchment.

"And my mother was a Christian!" exclaimed Laon impulsively; "it was for this that she was banished from her home and from Athens; for this that men speak of her as though she were vile. O mother, my mother! where art thou? let me find thee, that I may tell thee that thy God shall be my God. Thou wilt teach me to know and love him," he added, turning to the Christian preacher and bursting into tears.

The two old men had listened to his passionate outburst in wondering surprise, but the old Christian rose from his seat, and spreading his hands over Laon's bowed head, he said slowly, "The blessing of thy mother's God be upon thee! May he give thee richly of his grace and favor! May he lead and guide thee in every step thou takest, and bring thee at last to meet her at the feet of Jesus on the eternal shore!"

Laon lifted his head as he finished this benediction. "Didst thou know my mother?" he asked.

The old man shook his head. "She was doubtless one of the Lord's hidden ones here in Athens," he said.

"Then thou canst not tell me where she is—whither she was banished?" said Laon sadly.

"Nay, my son, but the Lord is with her wherever she may be."

"I, too, must find her," said Laon; "but I would learn somewhat more of thy religion first," he added.

Far into the night did the old man sit expounding the good news Paul had first brought to Athens, and each word seemed to fall as good seed in a prepared soil, and before they retired to rest Laon and Arnobius had determined to join the poor and despised sect of Nazarenes.

With the dawn of the day their teacher departed, that he might be in time to appear before the prefect on behalf of his brethren taken in the market-place. He declined the company of either Laon or his host.

"It may be ye were not recognized in the fray yesterday, and it would be unwise to cast yourselves into the jaws of the lion needlessly," he said; and so, after walking with him to the gate of the city while Arnobius scattered the fodder for the goats and put up their own food for the day, Laon came back to help his master with what they had to take to the market.

They both felt anxious to know how the prefect would deal with the prisoners, and, in spite of the old man's caution, Arnobius left the market soon after the stall was arranged, and, mingling with the crowd of gossips who were going to hear the decision of their Roman judge and governor, passed in without being recognized as the one who had helped several Nazarenes to escape.

There was, of course, a great deal of contradictory evidence as to the cause of the outbreak, but all agreed that it was upon the matter of religion that there had been so much fighting, the Athenians alleging that these vain babblers were followers of one Paul, who had introduced a new God into Athens, without permission of the Senate, about ten years before. The Jews were far more bitter than the Athenians in their complaints. "These people were followers of an apostate who had appeared in Judea and perished miserably as a slave and a malefactor," they said; "and in spite of this they taught that he had risen from the dead and was their only king, thus denying the power of the emperor."

The prefect looked puzzled when the name of the emperor was mentioned, but at length he said: "Ye Jews and men of Athens, it seemeth to me that ye know not the laws of Rome by which this province is now governed. Every nation hath gods of its own, and men of that nation are free to worship them. Ye Jews worship your God, whom ye call Jehovah, without let or hinderance from Roman law; therefore, these Nazarenes are free to worship Jesus Christ, so that the emperor receive not damage."

"Nay, but these Nazarenes are not content with the worship of their God, but speak evil of the others, calling them demons and idols, and saying that their God is to be worshiped of all nations."

"Nay, nay, but they are not so arrogant," said the prefect, trying to make peace. "To every nation its own god—Apollo and Jupiter for Rome and Athens, and—"

"Nay, nay, but our God is the God of the whole earth," said the Christian preacher boldly, and he proceeded to address the prefect and all that were assembled, until the Jews began to create another disturbance, when all were severely reprimanded, and threatened if another breach of the peace occurred they should be severely punished. After which the prisoners were set at liberty and the court broke up, the Nazarenes thankful for the toleration of their judge, and the Jews murmuring against him for encouraging this new sect.

CHAPTER XVII.

THE MEETING.

LEPIDA came back weary, sad, and disappointed, and Laon was not less so when he heard that she had not been able to find Glaucia.

"My errand was altogether a failure," she added; "I could do little in the business I went upon, and it seemed as though the very gods were against me."

She had sat down wearily in the porch, and had not yet entered the house to see the despite that had been done to her household and national deities in her absence, and Laon was too much absorbed in thoughts of his sister to remember these now. A short time afterward, however, she went into the kitchen, and the next minute a half-suppressed cry of horror rang through the house.

Laon hurried in-doors in alarm, but in a moment saw what had caused Lepida's trouble, for she was standing before the statues of her deities in bewildered surprise and horror.

Lepida's Horror at the Insult Offered to her Gods.

"Who—who has done this?" she asked in a hoarse whisper as Laon came in.

He hardly knew what to answer, for he did not know whether Arnobius intended to inform his wife of his change of faith at once, and so he said, in some perplexity, "Lepida, my mother did not believe in these gods; she was a Christian."

The woman started and looked at him earnestly. "Where hast thou been to discover this?" she asked. "Thou hast followed me to Corinth," she suddenly added.

"Nay, I have been to the agora each day with Arnobius," said Laon; "but I have learned to read, and the parchment thou gavest me was a message from the Christian's God."

"And the gods in anger have turned their faces from one who dared to read the message of another god," said Lepida, glancing at the statues.

Laon could not forbear a smile. "Nay, nay, but we turned them to the wall to see if they were gods enough to show their faces again without our help," he said.

Lepida was too angry and frightened to notice the light tone in which this was said, but when Arnobius returned she warned him never to leave Laon in the house alone again, as she feared some heavy calamity would already follow his daring act of impiety.

"Nay, nay, but the boy is not to blame for this fancied insult to Ceres and Pan. *I* turned them round," said her husband boldly.

"Thou!" uttered Lepida. "What could lead thee to be so daring and so profane, Arnobius?" she asked in an angry tone.

She had less patience with her husband than with Laon, and for a long time she refused to be pacified, refused even to sit down in a room where her gods had been insulted, and Arnobius had the truth and sincerity of his convictions put to a severe test by the bitter reproaches and tearful protestations of his wife.

At length the matter was settled by the old man consenting to let the national and family gods occupy their accustomed places, provided Lepida did not perform any act of worship in his presence, and, at the same time, leaving him free to serve the God of his choice. This, of course, involved the necessity of his being absent at the commencement of every meal, and it was easy to see that domestic happiness was at an end for both Arnobius and his wife.

Laon could not help seeing the coolness that had suddenly arisen between the two. Lepida went about her work in a fashion that seemed to say she believed it was all in vain, that some dread calamity must befall them ere long, while Arnobius studiously absented himself from every act of worship. At the same time, he studied his wife's comfort and convenience more carefully in other matters than he had ever done before.

Each day when he came home from the market he brought her some trifle as a proof of his affectionate thoughtfulness for her, and they were accepted gratefully; yet still it was easy to see that one libation poured to the lares and penates, one scrap of incense burned to Ceres or Pan, would have afforded her more satisfaction than all the gifts in the world. And so the days and weeks slipped by, Laon still helping Arnobius in the market, and listening by turns to the sermons preached at the entrance of the agora.

Sometimes the old preacher would stay at their stall for a few minutes to give them a word of counsel, or tell them when and where there would be a meeting of the brethren for prayer and instruction, for both Laon and his master had decided to join the Christian Church here in Athens. From this circumstance people had begun to guess that the old fruit-seller was a Nazarene and Laon likewise.

The Jews had not entered the market much since the riot, until one morning a number of them came in very early, and stationed themselves behind the pillars and inside the booths in such a manner that Arnobius and Laon were both convinced that another riot was impending.

"Run, Laon, and warn our teacher that he come not to the market to-day," said Arnobius, as he noticed how several fierce-looking Jews had gathered round a narrow passage by which they had managed to escape the last time.

Laon needed no second bidding to do this. He went with all speed to the home of the humble teacher of the Gospel, and finding he had already gone out to visit the angel or minister of the Church, Dionysius, he sped on there as fast as he could, and met the old man even then on the steps ready to depart for his daily work in the agora. When he heard Laon's tidings, however, he again entered the house of Dionysius to give him warning likewise of the impending danger; for these Christians, brave though they were, had begun to learn that it was of little use to preach to an angry mob, and so Laon had little difficulty in persuading him to keep out of the way.

When Laon got back to the market, however,

an unforeseen trouble awaited him. During his absence Arnobius had been accused of sending to warn the Nazarene not to come, and just as Laon appeared one of the most violent struck the old man such a blow that it felled him to the ground, while, at the same time, the blood flowed from a severe cut on his forehead.

Laon screamed for help, and a crowd soon began to gather round; but seeing the Jews near, and hearing the cause of the disturbance every body was afraid to help, until two young slaves came up to see what had happened. One of them was blind, but she managed to push her way through the crowd of her countrymen gathered near, and Glaucia kept so close beside her that, looking round, Laon saw both girls at once.

"Glaucia! Glaucia!" was all he could say as he gently laid down the old man's head and clasped his sister in his arms.

She was too much overcome to speak a word, but lay panting and sobbing in his arms, while Drusilla inquired of the bystanders the cause of the disturbance.

One or two of the Jews slunk away as Laon and Glaucia met, and their example was followed by others, and then some of the market people gathered courage enough to bind up the old man's wound and give him some restorative to bring him to himself again. In a few minutes he opened his eyes and saw Laon and Glaucia bending over him, while his head rested in Drusilla's lap, who was still bathing his temples.

"My children!" he said in a bewildered tone, looking from one to another.

"This is Glaucia," said Laon eagerly. He had not noticed Drusilla sufficiently to recognize her before, but he did so now, and bowed in lowly reverence before her.

"Arnobius, here is one who was honored by ministering to the noble Paul. I met her in Rome, but thought not to see her in our Athens."

A faint color stole into the blind girl's face, for Laon's words were even more surprising than his presence. "You showed me kindness in Rome," she managed to say at last.

"Nay, but thy kindness to me was greater than mine to thee, for thou wast the first to tell me of a God greater than Jupiter. Yes, Glaucia, and kinder then Pallas Athene," said Laon, looking affectionately at his sister.

"Yes, the God who has heard my prayers and taught thee to love himself," said Glaucia in a whisper.

Laon looked at his sister for one moment as if he scarce credited the evidence of his senses,

"Thou knowest this God too, Glaucia!" he uttered. "Then we will go in search of our mother together, and tell her that both her children are Christians."

"Thou art forgetting, Laon, that I am a slave," said Glaucia quickly.

He had forgotten every thing in the joy of seeing her once more—forgotten that they were in the market, where curious eyes were watching them and many ears were listening to the dangerous words they uttered. Glaucia came to a realization of this fact before her brother.

"I must not stay here," she said; "my mistress will be angry if I tarry too long."

"Thy mistress!" repeated Laon; "true, I had forgotten that my sister was a waiting-maid. Thou must be careful not to offend her, Glaucia," he said with sudden energy. "I have heard that these Roman ladies are cruel to their slaves, that the punishment they receive is—is—" he stopped; he could not tell Glaucia of that horrible spectacle as it rose before his mental vision, and she was in too great a hurry to depart to ask him any thing further.

She glanced at Arnobius as they raised him to a seat beside the stall, and then said in a whisper, "Art thou this old man's slave, Laon?"

"Nay, nay, this is our Lepida's husband, who

has befriended me. I escaped from the man who held us in bondage, and went in search of thee, and followed thee to Athens, and now that I have found thee I will free thee," he added, in a tone of joyous confidence.

Glaucia could not but look joyful too, but she took Drusilla's hand and hastened away, for they had already been a long time in the market, and Valeria might need her attendance, and she remembered that she had already offended her mistress. She told Laon something of this as he walked by her side through the street toward home, for he was loth to leave her so soon; and Arnobius had declared he was quite able to mind the stall, and that he had better go with his sister or Lepida would not be pleased. So they walked together through the streets of Athens, with the blind girl by their side, until the stately mansion of the Gracchi was reached, and then once more the brother and sister had to part.

"But only until to-morrow," said Laon. "Thou wilt come to the market to-morrow, Glaucia?"

"I will if I can, but thou must not forget I am a slave," she said, trying to smile as she spoke.

"Thou shalt not be a slave long, Glaucia,"

said Laon quickly, almost fiercely. "I have a plan by which I hope to redeem thee next spring," and with these parting words of comfort he hurried away, while Glaucia and Drusilla went in-doors, both feeling as though the events of the last hour must be the creation of some strange dream from which they should awake to the reality all too soon.

Meanwhile Laon had hurried back to the market, thinking of the change that seemed to have passed over his sister since they had been separated. She was a child then, clinging to him with all a child's timidity of helplessness, but now it seemed she was a woman, with her quiet, grave way of talking; and then he fell to wondering how it was Drusilla was with her, and whether she had taught her this Christian faith.

From Drusilla to his former friend Appius, the gladiator, was an easy transition, and he wished the emperor was coming sooner than the spring, for he longed to buckle the heavy cestus on his hand and try his skill in using it, for he had quite resolved to enter the lists and free Glaucia by means of the reward.

When he reached the market he found Arnobius slowly packing up his goods ready to return home. "I don't feel quite equal to contending for a pine-leaf crown in an Isthmian game, and so we will go home to Lepida and tell her thou hast found thy sister," said the old man with a faint smile.

Laon saw that he was more bruised and shaken than he cared to own, and so he readily agreed to reload the mule and go home again, although they had served very few customers that morning. On their way there he ventured to tell Arnobius his plan for redeeming his sister, and the old man rubbed his hands with delight and quite applauded the undertaking.

"I ran in the Isthmian games when I was young," said the old man, "and though the prize was a simple wreath of pine leaves that would fade in an hour instead of a sister's freedom, I thought little of the training that was needful to fit me for a competitor."

"And didst thou gain the prize?" asked Laon eagerly.

"Nay, nay, there were many competitors but only one crown," said Arnobius, "and I was not able to reach the goal first."

"And all the training was in vain, then," said Laon.

"Nay, not quite in vain; I had learned to keep under my body—to bear hunger and fatigue without flinching," said Arnobius, "and thou wilt have to do the same, doubtless, to join in this Roman game, if thou hopest to win the prize."

"I must and will win the prize," said Laon; "Glaucia must be freed, and I am the only one to do it."

A few weeks earlier they would both have stopped at the temple of Fortuna on their way home to propitiate the goddess, but now Arnobius only wished him success in a few hearty words, at the same time saying,

"I will ask counsel, my son, whether we may not pray to our God on this matter even as we should once have done to our goddess."

Arnobius, himself, evidently had no objection to the games of the arena, which was no small comfort to Laon, as he could now talk freely to him upon this all-absorbing topic as he could not to his nurse.

When they reached home Lepida met them at the door, looking pale and frightened. "It has begun," she murmured as she saw her husband's head with a blood-stained bandage around it.

"What has begun?" asked Arnobius.

"The vengeance of the gods," said Lepida. "I feared it would be so," she added.

"Nay, it was not the gods but the Jews who inflicted this wound," said Arnobius, with a faint smile.

"Then it is known in the market that thou art a Nazarene," said Lepida, with whitening lips.

"Yes, it is known, I doubt not," said Arnobius; "but forget that awhile, Lepida," he added, "Laon will be in directly, and he hath some news for thee."

His wife, however, took no notice of this. "O the disgrace that hath fallen upon me!" she wailed. "Would that Jupiter had smote this messenger, Paul, before he came to our Athens, for he hath shadowed all my life. The first victim was pure and noble as Juno herself, and this did but hasten her ruin it seemed; and now there is my Arnobius, the most honest fruit-seller in the agora, he has taken this evil plague of atheism."

She was interrupted at this point by the entrance of Laon. "My Lepida," he cried, "I have found Glaucia! she came to the market to-day, and she is—" but there he stopped. It was a pity to dampen the poor woman's joy by what she would think such evil tidings, and in her delight she did not notice how abruptly he left off speaking.

"My Glaucia is found—found at last!" she repeated over and over again, and before she went to bed she decided not to wait for a chance meeting with the girl, but to go boldly to the house and ask to see her, if only for a few moments.

CHAPTER XVIII.

PERSECUTION.

GLAUCIA stood in her little laboratory, where so many unguents, cosmetics, and perfumes were prepared for her mistress's use. A small marble basin stood before her in which she was pounding barley-meal, honey, and goats' milk with attar of roses into a sort of soap; but it was evident she was thinking of other things than those by which she was surrounded, and it seemed impossible to get her preparation of the right consistency to-day, and she heaved a deep sigh as she took a little more meal from the jar standing close at hand.

"I wonder what it is Laon fears," she whispered softly to herself. "He seems anxious and uneasy since I told him Valeria was still very angry with me. Will she punish me very severely, I wonder? Drusilla only shakes her head when I try to talk to her about it. She wishes they were going to stay here all the winter instead of going to Corinth to visit the deaconess, Phœbe, whom Paul is anxious to hear of. I wonder whether she thinks my punishment will begin when she is gone."

Glaucia mixed and pounded as she thus talked, but her work progressed very slowly, for it needed a little more honey, and now and then more perfume had to be added. Presently the curtain was lifted, and Drusilla came carefully stepping in among her jars and vases.

"Glaucia is at work, I know," said the blind girl. "Are we alone?" she asked in a whisper, after cautiously listening for a minute or two.

"Yes; Fulvia hath gone to the market today," said Glaucia with something of a sigh.

Several weeks had passed since she first saw Laon, and she had been allowed to go out but twice since. Fulvia had been sent on all the business to the market, and she had not been able to see her friend, the old Nazarene, at all. Laon, however, had taken a message for her to him, and likewise a request to Dionysius, the angel of the Church at Athens; for, taught by Drusilla and her noble mistress, Julia, the slave-girl was anxious to be recognized as a sister by being admitted as a member of the Church.

The visit of the noble Roman lady had greatly strengthened the faith and hope of the little company by the news she brought of the imprisoned Paul, for she had sought them out as soon as she arrived, and had met with them frequently for prayer. She had often spoken of Glaucia, too, who bore her captivity so patiently that no fault could be found with her by her mistress, excepting for her continued refusal to worship the gods of Rome again, so that a deep interest was felt for her, and many prayers ascended to the throne of grace on her behalf, although she knew nothing of it. The Roman lady often wondered, too, how she came to be possessed of that little parchment-roll that had slipped out of her bosom the first time she saw her. She wondered, too, whether she possessed it still, but she did not ask; indeed, Valeria took care that Glaucia had no opportunity of seeing their visitor often, and so the words of cheer and comfort she longed to speak to the desolate girl had to be sent through Drusilla.

As Glaucia surmised, she did fear that some heavy punishment would be inflicted upon her as soon as she left, and so, hoping that time would soften Valeria toward her little waiting-maid, she prolonged her visit far into the winter, although she had likewise promised to spend some time at Corinth before returning to Rome.

Claudia had gone back to her duties, leaving her friend sadly disappointed that she had not sought further into Divine truth, and been more brave than thus to return to a vain service. She had wanted Julia to sell Drusilla to her, that she might have some one at hand should she ever be seized with sickness again, but this the lady refused to do. The little Jewess was not only a faithful servant, but a sister in Christ, and therefore she dare not expose her to such temptations as must await her in such a service as Claudia's, even for the doubtful benefit of further enlightening her mind.

Another thing Julia could see—that Drusilla was a help to Glaucia, who had such a hard battle to fight, such an unequal conflict to maintain, in this idolatrous family. All the household knew that she had forsaken the worship of the gods; it was not possible to conceal the fact for a single day and be faithful to the command of God. Each time the threshold was crossed, each meal that was placed on the table, almost every department of household work, called for its special act of worship to its presiding divinity. Literally and really, whether they ate or drank, or whatsoever they did, must be done to the glory of one of the host of deities; and so each omission was reckoned as an insult, and Glaucia was treated as an outcast, despised, and often ill-treated, by her fellow slaves, while the epithets "Nazarene" and "Christian" served as an excuse for giving her as much extra work as was possible, and all this her mistress did not or would not see. She never spoke to her, now, except to give a command or find some fault with the way she arranged her hair or prepared the bath; and the poor girl often looked pale, weary, and disheartened in spite of the calm, restful peace that seemed to shine in her face. It was little to be wondered at, therefore, that she clung to the hope of release Laon had given her. But for this, and her firm faith in the love and power of God, she must have yielded when one and another of her companions tried to persuade her to sacrifice to the gods again.

There was one, however, who never joined in these persuasions, or the little persecutions she had to suffer; for Felicita herself, more than half convinced of the truth of that religion that could bear such beautiful fruit as that she had seen at Corinth, silently admired the quiet bravery of the usually timid girl in so steadily holding to her principles in spite of all opposition. She was afraid she should not be so firm; and yet the religion that could give such strength of endurance had a great fascination for her, and she sometimes ventured to ask Glaucia some questions when they were by themselves; and more than once she ventured to kneel down in prayer to God.

So the weeks had slipped by since Glaucia's return, and midwinter, with its feast to Saturn, that every slave looked forward to with such delight, was drawing near. Glaucia remembered what a holiday this used to be in her old home. Every room in the house was decorated with evergreens, and dancing and revelry was the order of the day. Not only for the rich, but for the poorest slave of the household, it was a season of rejoicing, when they enjoyed more liberty than they did all the rest of the year—a liberty that often went to the excess of license. Visits were paid and received, and Glaucia began to look forward to this glad season, when she hoped she should be able to pay a visit to Lepida, and spend some hours with her and Laon.

She had talked to Drusilla about this, and the blind girl, who had learned to find her way to the market by herself, had talked to Laon about it too, and had carried sundry messages backward and forward between them. She was a discreet messenger, and kept the secrets of both when she knew it would give pain to reveal every thing, and so Laon knew very little of what his sister was suffering, for Glaucia had made Drusilla promise she would not tell him any thing beyond the bare fact that her mistress would not allow her to come to the market now.

That, however, was bad enough, he thought, and he confided to Drusilla, under a promise of secrecy not to tell his sister, how Lepida and he had both called at the house to see Glaucia and been refused each time, although Lepida had made several journeys to Athens on purpose.

"Never mind, the saturnalia is coming, and then you will have a happy time together," said Drusilla; "and my mistress says it would be well for thee and Glaucia to be admitted to the Church then, as thou art wishing the admission to be at the same time as thy sister's."

"Yes, I will wait for Glaucia," said Laon, "and I hope that very soon she will be able to go to each meeting of the Church. Hast thou heard that the emperor purposes visiting Corinth and Athens next spring?" he asked.

"Yes, my mistress spoke of it, for we are going to visit the Church of Corinth, and she would fain leave before the emperor arrives, because the city will be so full of visitors," said Drusilla; but she raised her sightless eyes to his face, as though she did not comprehend why this should interest him so much.

He understood the look. "The coming of the emperor will enable me to free Glaucia," he said, and then he explained what he intended to do.

But, to his surprise, Drusilla appeared any thing but pleased, and at last she said, "Laon, thou must not do this."

"Must not do it! Why?" uttered Laon.

"Thou art a Christian," said the blind girl slowly, "and the games of Rome, like those of Greece, are of the world, that is, enmity against God. Thou wouldst not join the enemies of God," she said.

"It is not because I love the games of the arena, but to save Glaucia," said Laon quickly. "Surely it cannot be wrong to want to save my sister," he added.

"It would be wrong if thou, her brother, did not try to free her, since thou thyself art free," said Drusilla, "but the way thou art proposing to do it is wrong."

"But it is for a great good, even the freedom of my sister, I would do it," said Laon earnestly.

For a minute or two the girl looked puzzled

by this argument, but at last she said, "No, Laon, it cannot be any thing but evil, for I heard from the epistle of our great teacher that we may not sin that grace may abound, or that good may come, and so—and so—" she did not finish her speech, for she knew how deeply disappointed Laon would feel.

How bitterly he felt it she did not know. To have this hope taken from him was taking all the zest from life—was dooming him to a slavery worse almost than his sister's, for how could he enjoy any thing while she was a slave. Even the religious service, so helpful, so strengthening to his faith, would cease to be a joy and delight when he reflected that Glaucia would be shut out.

Laon turned away silently and sadly, and Drusilla went home feeling scarcely less sad, for how could she tell Glaucia that the hope she clung to so fondly was but as a rope of sand; and yet she felt that Glaucia herself must decide this question, or Laon would not give up his meditated attempt.

Of the danger he incurred, of the possibility that he might be killed, and thus leave his sister hopelessly enslaved, she never once thought. The attempt was in itself wrong—a sin in the sight of God; and no success and no good that might follow could ever make it otherwise, and therefore it was Drusilla's duty to prevent it if possible. So she went in search of Glaucia as soon as she reached home, carefully asking if they were alone. She noticed the sigh that followed Glaucia's announcement of Fulvia having gone to the market, and the tears rose to her eyes as she thought of the task that was before her, but she tried to speak cheerfully.

"I have been to the market," she said as she seated herself in the corner.

Glaucia left off mixing her cosmetic. "Thou hast seen Laon," she said; and then, noticing the look of distress in Drusilla's face, she asked anxiously, "Has any thing happened? Is he quite well?"

"Yes, he is quite well," answered Drusilla.

But Glaucia was not satisfied. "What is it? what has happened?" she asked.

For answer the blind girl kissed her cheek fondly, at the same time whispering, "Our Lord Christ said, that all who were his disciples must take up the cross and follow him."

"I am not worthy, but I am trying so to follow my loving Lord," answered Glaucia.

"And he who gives the cross gives the strength to bear it," whispered the blind girl.

Glaucia bowed. "Even so," she said, and then she added, "but thou hast something more to tell me—some evil tidings, Drusilla."

"Couldst thou give up any thing thou art possessed of for the sake—at the bidding—of the Lord Christ?" asked Drusilla.

"Nay, I possess nothing," answered Glaucia. "The Lord hath taken my empty heart and filled it with his love, and I—I have nothing to give but this love, his own gift, in return."

"But suppose the Lord should ask thee to give thy life for him, or something almost as dear as life," said Drusilla.

Glaucia turned a shade paler, but she said in a calm voice, "The Lord Christ gave his life for mine, therefore it is no longer mine, but his. Hast thou heard what my punishment is to be?" she added.

"Thy punishment!" repeated Drusilla.

"Yes; Valeria told me this morning I should yet be punished for my obstinacy," said Glaucia, "and thou hast come to tell me what it is."

"Nay, I have not heard a word concerning thy punishment," answered the blind girl. "I have just returned from the market."

"Then it is something concerning Laon," said Glaucia quickly. "O tell me what it is!" she added. "I can bear any thing for myself, but for my brother—" and she stopped, for there came a choking sensation in her throat at the thought of trouble coming to him.

"Yes, it is something concerning Laon and thee too," said Drusilla. "Didst thou know *how* he proposed redeeming thee?" she asked.

"Nay, he told me it was a secret," replied Glaucia.

"Yes, and a great sin," said the blind girl firmly.

Glaucia started. "The Lord Christ hath redeemed my soul with his own blood, my body must not be redeemed by sin," she said. "But—but Laon is a Christian too," she added; "he would not do evil even for me."

"He thought not of its being evil," said Drusilla, "he thought only of the prize—the bag of sesterces that would redeem thee."

"And what would he do to gain this bag of sesterces?" asked Glaucia.

"Fight as a gladiator in the arena."

Glaucia had heard of the Isthmian and Olympic games, but the arena, with its savage spectacles of wild beasts fighting with almost equally brutal men, or the men fighting with each other until the death of one put an end to the sport, was not known in Greece, and the family in which she lived being more Grecian than Roman in their habits, the word "gladiator" had to be explained to her, and from her long residence in Rome Drusilla was able to do this.

Glaucia shuddered as she heard of the bloody, brutal fights, but she said quickly, "Laon would not do this."

"Not to please himself but to free thee," said Drusilla.

"Nay, nay, but I cannot be ransomed at such a cost," she said with a shudder. "What! have a man killed that I might be free! Nay, slavery would be far, far better. And, then, if it should be Laon who was killed and the other gained the prize—O Drusilla, thou hast told him it must not be!" she added earnestly.

"Yes, I told him it was wrong—a sin against God—but I know not whether he felt it to be so, and that is why I talked to thee that thou mayest persuade him to give up the plan."

"O that I could see him and tell him what I think, what I feel about this!" she exclaimed. "Drusilla, thou must go again to the market to-morrow and tell him that I am grieved, distressed, that I cannot be redeemed by this means; tell him I will wait—"

"Wait the Lord's time," interrupted Drusilla. "We will kneel and ask him to help

Laon yield up his own way, and give him faith to believe that he can set thee free at the right time." And, securing the curtain with a loop and clasp, the two girls kneeled down and poured out their trouble before God, and then Drusilla went and told her mistress all that had happened.

CHAPTER XIX.

LIGHT AT EVENTIDE.

THE saturnalia had begun, and Athens was alive with gay revelers. Care, trouble, and anxiety were for the time forgotten, and the most hard-worked slave put on some appearance of joy and festivity.

The household of Fabrizzio Gracchi were no exception, although their master lay dying, for every slave except Glaucia had some share in the seven days' revelry; but for her there was no change, no holiday; nothing was to be allowed to break the monotony of her life. This was to be her punishment. If she would not worship the gods she was to have no relaxation from toil when their festivals came round, and, as only the small band of Christians observed the first day of the week as a day of rest, life had no sabbaths for Glaucia, it was all one long, monotonous, working day.

Lepida and Laon were almost as much disappointed as Glaucia herself, for they were not allowed to see her, although Fulvia had her friends to visit her, besides being allowed to visit them, for Valeria contrived to give every one extra liberty, and setting Glaucia to do their work.

She was even left in attendance on her father while the usual slave went out, a change of nurses that did not escape the philosopher's notice, for, looking at Glaucia one day, he said:

"How is it thou art so obstinate? Thou dost not look like one who could be willfully bad."

Glaucia colored. "I am striving to live blamelessly, as becometh a follower of one so holy and pure as the Lord Christ," she said in a gentle tone.

"The Lord Christ!" repeated the philosopher; "that is he whom Julia talked of, and she once said something about his resurrection. Is it true that he rose from the dead?"

"Yes," said Glaucia; "he appeared to many of his disciples, talked with them, and ate with them, as he had done before his death, and afterward ascended up into heaven in their sight."

"And the writings of your religion treat of such lofty themes as these!" exclaimed the philosopher. "I would that I had heard of it earlier, that I might have compared it with the writings of Plato; but it is too late now—too late," he repeated sadly.

"Nay, nay; but it needeth not wisdom or learning to come to the Lord Christ," said Glaucia, her master's need giving her boldness to speak out all she knew.

"But I am too near the land of shades to examine this new religion now," said Fabrizzio with a sigh.

"Nay; but, if thou art seeking the light, and would fain turn from the darkness of the grave, Christ will give thee light. He is himself the light," said Glaucia earnestly. And in simple language, such as she would use if talking to Laon or Drusilla, she told the world-wise philosopher the story of the life and death of Christ, and how he had brought life and immortality to light.

Gradually the dim eyes brightened, and a look of intense interest overspread the pallid, wasted face; and when at length his wife came in and would have sent Glaucia away, he begged her to leave her with him still.

"The child amuses me," he said by way of excuse, seeing his wife's look of amazement.

A little later Valeria came, and, pausing at the entrance, was startled to hear her father say: "Thou art sure He will receive an old man who has wearied himself in searching for some light to shine on this darkness, but ever despised this sect of Nazarenes?"

What Glaucia's answer was she could not hear, for she was kneeling beside the couch, and it was in a low, reverent voice, almost in the tones of supplication, she was speaking.

Presently there came another question: "Hath thy God no image, no statue, nothing by which we can worship him?"

"No," answered Glaucia; "no image, no statue even by Phidias, could shadow forth his love or his power; and he has forbidden us the use of graven images, or to worship any thing as the likeness of himself."

"And that is why thou refusest to sacrifice to the gods?" asked her master.

"It would be a grief and an insult to the Lord Christ if I gave his glory to a graven image," said Glaucia gently.

A slight noise gave them notice of Valeria's entrance, and Glaucia retired to the further end of the room as the lady came forward.

"Shall I read to thee, my father?" she asked.

"What canst thou read?" asked the philosopher.

Valeria looked up in surprise. "We have not finished all the writings of Plato," she said.

" Valeria, husks will not feed a hungry man," said the invalid; and I am a hungered for the knowledge thy slave Glaucia possesses. I would that I had talked to Julia of this before she left for Corinth."

"She only left yesterday," said Valeria mechanically, and with a faint smile. She was thinking how useless all her precautions had been to keep Julia from him for fear she should introduce the subject of her religion, and she should utter in his hearing the words that had haunted her ever since they had been spoken. She wondered now whether Glaucia had told him of this "life and immortality brought to light."

She was not left long in doubt. "There is a life beyond the grave, and this new faith reveals it," said the philosopher. "I must know how I can attain it before I die," he added, looking earnestly at his daughter.

She hardly knew what to do or what to say. Was her father's mind unhinged through his long illness? Surely it must be so or he would not speak thus.

His next words, however, were more alarming still. "The leader of this sect in Athens is a learned citizen, named Dionysius, dwelling near the western gate; wilt thou send for him,

Valeria, and ask him to bring the writings of his religion, that he may set my doubts at rest?"

Valeria dared not refuse her father's request, and yet to ask such a man to cross their threshold would compromise the family honor so deeply that she shrank from doing it as long as possible, wondering whom she could send, for the slaves would be sure to talk of it among themselves, and they might so exaggerate the matter that it might be said that her father had forsaken the gods before he died.

Thinking thus, she went to consult her mother, who was more inclined to treat the matter as a sick man's whim than her daughter; but knowing that it must be gratified, since her husband had set his heart upon it, she counseled that Glaucia should be sent with a letter to Dionysius desiring his presence, and she took out her waxen tablets at once and wrote the request. Binding it with a silken cord, Glaucia was dispatched with it to Dionysius, Valeria and her mother both hoping that the minister might not be at home, or would refuse to come. But Dionysius, though surprised at the message, promised to follow Glaucia at once, and, indeed, he arrived almost as soon as she got back.

The ladies were courteous, but received him coldly, Romola stating that it was but to gratify a sick man's whim that she had requested his presence, as she conducted him to her husband's bedside.

Dionysius bowed, but did not reply, for the sick-chamber was reached, and the next minute the minister of Christ stood beside the invalid.

The eager, anxious gaze of those earnest gray eyes was in itself a refutation of his wife's assertion, and time was now too precious to be wasted in apologies and mere forms of politeness.

"Thou hast come to tell me of Christ, the light of the world?" said the philosopher as his visitor seated himself beside the couch.

"Yes, that is the highest wisdom man can attain unto in this life," said Dionysius.

"And I have been searching for it all my life," said the philosopher, "stretching weary hands into the darkness."

"Striving to reach the Unknown God by the help of this world's wisdom," said Dionysius.

"How else should he be sought for?" asked the invalid.

"Even as thou art seeking him now, weary and heavy laden, as a tired child seeks its mother's arms for rest."

"Rest!" repeated the philosopher. "Can thy God give rest? Can he satisfy the wants of our craving hearts, when the host of deities we possess fail to do so?"

"Yes, for our God made these hearts of ours and created the longings and cravings within them, on purpose that we might be satisfied with nothing but himself."

"But all the longings, all the cravings," said the philosopher. "One God could not combine all the attributes of our Olympian deities in himself."

"Yes, He is infinite, and therefore he can satisfy the wants of every heart, diverse as it may be. This is beyond our comprehension, and therefore man has made a host of gods, that each may worship the one answering best to his needs. One who longs for wisdom and knowledge bows to Pallas Athene; Jupiter claims the votary of power; Apollo the lover of music, poetry, and science; but the wants of all are met in the fullness of God our Creator. His heart is as the ocean, boundless; illimitable in power, purity, and love"

"Ah! our gods are not pure," said Fabrizzio. "I have turned from some in sickening disgust, for were they men they should not come within my atrium, and how, then, could I worship such?

I have longed for a purity and goodness above and beyond my own, as well as for light to shine upon the utter darkness of the land of shades."

"And our God is pure, with a spotlessness that rivals the crown of Hymettus; with a brightness that is beyond the blaze of the noonday sun. No shadow of evil has ever dimmed the luster of his holiness, and sin and impurity can never enter his presence."

"How, then, can mortal man essay to enter that kingdom beyond the funeral urn, where He reigns in person?" asked the philosopher. "There are follies of youth, and manhood and—"

"Nay, call them not follies, but sins," said the minister; "we have no Saviour for follies of youth; but for sin, we have a sin-bearer, God's equal and fellow, who through his mighty power became the Atlas for the sin of the world, taking it as a heavy burden upon his shoulder, and bearing it—every man's share of the horrible load—that he might go free. It is through him—Jesus Christ—we can enter this heavenly kingdom."

"And he, this God-man, has borne my sins!" exclaimed Fabrizzio. "What shall I pay him for this?"

"Nay, there is no payment to be made, only believe this record of His love—accept God's free gift of eternal life."

"But I would fain give the half—nay, the whole—of my wealth to Him."

"What is thy wealth to One who has created and owns all this world, as well as the brilliant stars in the heavens. Eternal life is God's free gift to rich and poor alike. All who enter heaven must lay down their pride on this side the gate, and walk in lowly, as little children."

The terms, so easy for the slave, were very hard to this rich, proud philosopher; and yet, while he demurred, his heart went out to this God, who was so holy and so pitiful, so great and so gracious.

"If He would only take a gift, a sacrifice, at my hands," said Fabrizzio; "but I have never accepted a favor in my life from the gods or men. I ever sacrificed freely to the one, and given gifts to the others, and I would fain do so even to the end."

"But it cannot be," said the minister. "Salvation must be accepted by thee upon the same terms as by thy little slave, Glaucia—without money and without price. God gives royally, as a king, and it were an insult to offer a king payment for his gifts."

"Yes," assented the philosopher; "and, humbling as the terms are, it is yet a joy and gladness to hear of this salvation."

"But a greater joy to accept it," said Dionysius, as he rose to take his departure. "I will come again to-morrow," he said, "if it will please thee to receive me; thou art growing weary now, and—"

"No, not weary; but I would fain be alone to ponder over the wonderful tidings thou hast brought," said the invalid. "Thou wilt come again to-morrow?" he added as his visitor left.

Romola thanked him for his visit, but did not ask him to repeat it, a fact Dionysius could not help noticing, although he resolved not to let it influence him, since there was one weary soul hungering for the words of eternal life; and so the next day he again presented himself at the door of the mansion, and was admitted before the ladies knew of his arrival, for Glaucia had seen him enter the atrium, and conducted him at once to her master's room.

Early as it was, Fabrizzio was anxiously expecting him, and welcomed him with a smile. "Hast thou brought the record thou spakest of yesterday?" he asked eagerly.

"Yes," answered the minister, drawing a roll of papyrus from his girdle. "This is the witness of one who went about with the Lord Christ, and saw his works of mercy when he was on earth;" and he began reading the account of the crucifixion, and then went on to that of the resurrection, adding but few words of his own to the sublimely simple account given by the apostle of these most wonderful events.

As he concluded, Fabrizzio laid his hand on his arm. "I do, I must believe," he said; "but will thy God receive me now? Will he take this weary, empty heart, and will he say to me, as to the malefactor, thou shalt be with me in paradise?"

"Yes, He is willing—waiting to receive thee; asking thee to be reconciled to himself," said Dionysius.

"It is wonderful—marvelous. I would that I could once more move among men to tell them of this wonderful love of God; but the shadow of death was upon me before this wonderful dawn arose: but thou wilt tell all men I died a believer in Christ—that the gods of Rome could not satisfy the sore hunger of my heart, and the philosophy of Greece was but as husks instead of bread. I will speak to my wife and daughter. Pray to thy God—to my God—for my Valeria; for I would that she, too, could accept this salvation."

He could not say any more, but lay back on his pillow exhausted, and Dionysius, looking at that pale, drawn face, could not but believe that the eternal day would soon break for the old man who had been seeking it in darkness all his life long. He knelt at the side of the couch and commended his soul in prayer to God, and then took an affectionate leave of his new convert.

"I am so weary, so tired, I want to rest—rest—rest," and, still murmuring the word, like a child sinking to sleep in its mother's arms, Fabrizzio closed his eyes, and Dionysius left the room. As he passed through the atrium and vestibule the slaves looked at him very curiously, wondering not a little what their master could want with this Nazarene, for one or two had recognized him as belonging to that disreputable sect, and had told their companions.

Neither of the ladies presented themselves to-day, and Dionysius passed out wondering whether he should ever see his new convert again. Seeing Glaucia, he told her to go and tell her mistress he had left, for he believed the angel of death was even then at the door, and he knew how anxious both wife and daughter would be to catch the last breath—the parting soul—of the beloved husband and father, and he judged truly that they would hasten to the chamber as soon as he had left.

Not one moment too soon was the message delivered. Romola hastened to her husband's side, not dreaming that the end was so near. He roused as she came in, and a calm smile rested on his face.

"The darkness is over at last, for I have found the light. Meet me in the land of light," he murmured, as his wife bent over him, and the next minute he was in the presence of God, so long unknown, so lately found.

CHAPTER XX.

A CLASSIC FUNERAL.

THE seven days of the saturnalia were not at an end when the solemn cypress bough was laid at the threshold of the door, and men knew, as they passed, that Fàbrizzio Gracchi was dead.

Dionysius saw it when he came the next day, and in spite of the coldness evinced by the ladies hitherto, he ventured to ask if he might see the corpse, hoping that he might likewise see the wife or daughter, and hear what had passed after he left. Permission was given him to view the corpse, and he went into the chamber where, bathed and anointed with the sweetest perfumes, the corpse lay on an ivory bed, arrayed in the richest festive robes.

Dionysius was disappointed to find that an old slave had taken the place of Romola to watch the corpse while he was there, for now he would have no opportunity of speaking that comfort the Christian religion alone could give. He knew that these mourners were sorrowing without hope, for the world beyond the grave was a dark, unknown mystery to them; but he could not force himself upon them now, and so, placing the amaranthine wreath he had brought on the cold brow of the corpse, he took his departure.

The sad offices to be performed while the corpse remained in the house, and the preparations for the funeral, occupied the time and attention of the whole household, and this was to Glaucia a time of rest and peace such as she had not known for some time; but she took no advantage of this, and beyond seeing Laon in the market once or twice, she had little change in her mode of life.

It was arranged that the funeral should take place just before sunset, for the Greeks, in their love of symbol and poetry, timed their funerals according to the age of the deceased, and Romola, taking into consideration her husband's age and his last words, wished that the last rays should shine upon the funeral pyre. So in the afternoon, when the market people were returning homeward after their day's work, the hired mourners and musicians left the stately mansion singing a solemn funeral dirge, that arrested every footstep in the grand old street. Then, as this was concluded, the body, placed on a bier covered with a purple pall, was carried out of the house, the mourners arranging themselves at either side, while the musicians went first, playing a slow, solemn march, to which the females kept time with their voices. In front of the corpse was carried his image, and those of his Roman ancestors; while close behind the bier walked the wife and daughter with bare, bowed heads and disheveled hair, making no moan, but grieving for their dead with a grief that we can never know, since we have the hope of meeting our beloved ones beyond the grave.

Slowly the funeral procession passed through the streets, all the slaves of the household bringing up the rear. The city gates were passed, and outside the walls the pyre of pine wood had been raised and covered with fragrant incense. On this the bearers placed the corpse, and then all stood aside at a respectful distance while the two mourners went to look their last on the husband and father, and place the death-penny in his mouth that was to pay the ferryman to row him over the fabled Styx, for not yet had the soul gained the land of shades, according to the popular belief. Romola pressed passionate kisses on the lips, eyes, and brow, and then, mechanically taking the torch from the priest of Jupiter, set fire to the pile. As the flames leaped up the mourners commenced singing a funeral dirge, and this announced to all that the sacred flame was wafting the soul to its destination.

As the ruddy flames shot up between the solemn cypress boughs that bent above them, the last rays of the setting sun fell across the face of the corpse, and Romola, with her daughter, turned away to sit apart in their agony of sorrow while the flames did their work, aided by the wind that came sweeping over the plain. At last it wavered, flickered, and then died out, and the last sparks were extinguished by the attendants, and then the embers were collected, and after being steeped in costly wine were placed in a silver urn, ready to be carried to Rome and placed in the family sepulcher. Until this could be done it was stored in a sepulcher close at hand. This was covered with flowers and wreaths, and hung round with lamps; and then the mourners, being purified by sprinkling from a bunch of laurel, slowly returned home under the darkling sky, feeling that they were indeed alone in a desolate world.

It was a matter of uncertainty now whether they would continue to reside at Athens or return to Rome; but at length the widow decided to remain until after the emperor's visit, which would not be until late in the spring, as he was going to Corinth first to witness the Isthmian games and to introduce his Roman gladiators.

Laon had been induced to relinquish his plan of going to Corinth and seeking Appius on his arrival, but what it cost him to do so no one knew. Glaucia herself had to persuade him, for it was hard for him to believe that the object he had in view would not sanctify the means used for its attainment. His friends among the Christian converts tried to make him see it as a sin in the sight of God, but their efforts were not wholly successful.

Laon had not long cast off the worship of his gods, and there had been little to try the sincerity of the change until now; but that he could resign this cherished project at all because of its being displeasing to God, was in itself a severe test to one of Laon's ardent temperament. Opposition, such as Glaucia had to encounter, would have been less of a trial than an opportunity for him to display the native energy and combativeness of his character; but to remain passive, and let this opportunity of redeeming his sister by one grand stroke slip by him forever—this was a trial indeed. Again and again, as the winter merged into spring, did the temptation arise to go to Corinth in spite of all that had been said ; and it was only after earnest prayer and many battles with his own self-will that he could resign this dearly-cherished plan.

Meanwhile Julia and Drusilla had reached Corinth, and, as they had anticipated, found the Christian Church there much larger and more flourishing than in the sister city of Athens. Phœbe the deaconess, who had labored with Paul himself in planting this infant Church, could relate how the polite scholar and learned Jewish Pharisee had worked at tentmaking with his own hands, in company with Aquila and Priscilla, for more than a year, while teaching and preaching to both Jews and Gentiles.

Julia was a most welcome visitor, for she brought news of their beloved teacher, and could tell them how the time of his imprisonment was passed in Rome ; how converts, even from among the rough soldiers and pleasure-loving courtiers of the emperor himself, had been added to the growing Church in Rome. She had likewise heard while in Athens that before the emperor paid his visit to Corinth he would sit in judgment on this famous Jewish prisoner that his countrymen felt so bitter against, so that his imprisonment would be at an end shortly, but what that end would be none could tell.

The Jewish proselyte, Poppæa, had great influence over Nero, and doubtless this would be used to secure Paul's condemnation; but even this was less to be feared than Nero's own cruel, ruthless disregard of the value of human life. When he first ascended the imperial throne his disposition was mild and amiable, the chief fault of his character being an inordinate vanity and love of pleasure; but he had gradually developed into a tyrant before whom the stoutest heart quailed, for he regarded nothing that stood in the way of his pleasure or opposed his despotic will; and since his own mother had fallen a victim to his cruelty, who could deem himself secure? So, in view of this coming trial, prayer was offered every day that God would spare his servant and deliver him from this lion.

From speaking of Paul and Rome, Julia talked of her lengthened stay in Athens, and then of Glaucia, and how bravely she was fighting the good fight of faith in the midst of an idolatrous family, and how disappointed her brother was, that, being a Christian, he could not enter the lists as a gladiator to free her. At the mention of Athens and the name of Glaucia, one of

Phœbe's fellow-helpers started, and a faint color stole into her pale cheek.

"Our Sister Hyrmina once lived in Athens!" explained Phœbe.

"And I had a little daughter named Glaucia, who is now in Rome with wealthy friends," said the lady with a deep-drawn sigh.

Phœbe knew the subject was a painful one to her friend, and turned the conversation to another subject; but Hyrmina sat with a look of deep concern on her face, and took but little interest in the remainder of the conversation. It was evident she was thinking more of the little slave-girl in Athens than of her great teacher in Rome, and she came to Phœbe the next day with a proposal that rather startled her, interfering, as she feared it would, with the concerns of the Athenian Church.

"But our brethren are poorer in Athens," said Hyrmina, "and this is not a matter of Church discipline, or relieving the necessities of their widows. We might make a collection here, and, without defrauding our own poor, release this girl from her cruel bondage."

"If it could be done I would gladly give a hundred sesterces," said the Roman lady, "for is she not our sister—one for whom Christ died?"

"I will give two hundred," said Hyrmina,

"and, moreover, find a trusty messenger to carry it to Dionysius to make the purchase of Valeria."

"The Church will doubtless gladly contribute the sum needful," said Phœbe; "it will be a thousand sesterces, I think thou saidst," she added, turning to Julia.

"A thousand was what Valeria paid for her," said Julia. And the next day, when the Church met together to pray for the deliverance of Paul, they were asked to contribute of their earthly goods for the deliverance of Glaucia.

A liberal response was made to this appeal, and before Julia left to return to Rome the whole sum was made up, and sent to Dionysius to transact the business of setting Glaucia free.

When the letter of the Corinthian Christians was read in the church of Athens every one rejoiced, not only that Glaucia would be rescued from her hard mistress, but for the liberality and sympathy this expressed.

Dionysius went at once to see Valeria, and ask the price she demanded for her little waiting-maid; while Laon hastened home to tell Lepida the joyful news. But, alas! the rejoicing was soon at an end. Valeria received the minister after several refusals, but, to his great sorrow, she positively refused to release Glaucia; she would not sell her for two thousand sesterces, she said.

In vain Dionysius pleaded her faithful service, and her refusal to worship the gods making it undesirable to retain her among the other slaves. Valeria was inexorable. They would return to Rome shortly, she said, and then she would find means of compelling Glaucia's obedience, and with this message he was obliged to return and acquaint the messenger from Corinth of the failure of his mission.

Laon's heart died within him when he heard the dreadful news, and again arose that awful spectacle before his vision which he had seen outside the city walls, and in his distress he went to Dionysius, telling him what he feared would be his sister's fate when she went back to Rome.

"Our Lord Christ, who himself tasted the agonies of such a death, can alone save her," said Dionysius sadly. "The Church will pray for her, and thou must do the same, even as our Brother Paul hath bidden us, saying, 'Be careful for nothing; but in every thing by prayer and supplication with thanksgiving let your requests be made known unto God.'"

And Laon did pray as he had never prayed

before—prayed with that cruel cross always before him, and with but one thought of comfort that the Lord Christ had tasted of this deeper depth of human agony and suffering, and therefore could sympathize with him in his fear, and with her likewise, if she was to glorify him by such a death.

What Laon was suffering on her account, or of the effort that had been made to redeem her, Glaucia knew nothing. She had heard from Fulvia and Felicita that they were to return to Rome shortly, and the preparations were nearly completed, when a messenger arrived from Rome bringing letters from Claudia and Julia, as well as to the Churches of Athens and Corinth. The news for the Churches was joyful indeed. Paul had been acquitted, and was at liberty; and hymns of praise resounded on every side for the deliverance God had wrought in answer to prayer.

The news received by Romola and Valeria, however, was any thing but gratifying, it seemed, and at once put an end to the preparations for their return to the imperial city, though what it was remained a secret for some time. At length orders were given for a room to be prepared for the reception of a lady, but the one chosen was as far as possible from Valeria's or her mother's, and it was furnished as plainly as possible.

A few days afterward Claudia arrived alone and unattended. Glaucia was in the peristyle with Valeria when she came in; but instead of going forward to greet her sister, she turned haughtily away.

"Show that lady to her room near the atrium," she said to Glaucia as she passed out to inform her mother of her sister's arrival.

Claudia stood still, almost gasping for breath, just where her sister had left her; but at last she saw Glaucia, and then remembering where she was, she said in a choking voice, "Wilt thou show me to my room?"

An angry flush suffused her cheek when she saw the chamber, and noticed that it joined the slaves' apartments.

"This is not fit for my father's daughter," she said; but the next minute, before Glaucia could reply, she had conquered her wounded pride, and said gently, "Never mind, I can perhaps be more comfortable here."

Glaucia helped her to unrobe, mentally asking what Claudia could have done to displease her mother and sister so much that she was to be treated little better than a servant in her own home; for while every luxury abounded in

Valeria's dressing-room, this was provided with the barest necessaries, and Glaucia had heard the order given to the cook to serve the expected guest at a small table in her own room, as she would not join the family meals. This, however, which Glaucia thought such a humiliation, seemed to please Claudia when she was told of the arrangement.

"I am quite content," she said. "Wilt thou ask if I may see my mother now?" she said, when the dust of travel had been removed and she had changed her dress.

Glaucia went to ask if she could be admitted to her mother's dressing-room, but brought back such a message that, instead of delivering it, the poor girl burst into tears when she reached Claudia's room.

"What is it?" said the lady, turning pale. "Does my mother refuse?" she asked.

"I am commanded to tell thee that—that thou hast no mother," said Glaucia in a hoarse whisper.

Claudia sank upon the couch near which she was standing, and covered her face with her hands for a few minutes. Then, lifting her head, she said, "Glaucia, thou art braver than I am, thou must pray for me, for Claudia the vestal is now Claudia the Christian."

CHAPTER XXI.

THE FIRST PERSECUTION.

ATHENS was doomed to disappointment in her expectation of entertaining the emperor this year 64, but what was a disappointment to others was a great relief to Romola and her eldest daughter, for the disgrace Claudia had brought upon the family name in forsaking her vows was felt most keenly, and the poor girl was made to suffer for it accordingly. Her condition was little better than Glaucia's; and it needed a faith as strong and a love and zeal as warm as they possessed who afterward gained a martyr's crown from the midst of the arena, to bear the little daily and hourly persecutions that were heaped upon her. Her mother and sister rarely spoke to her; and even when she ventured to ask for some particulars about her father's last hours, was abruptly told that as she had cut herself off from her family by the profession of this infamous faith, it could be of no moment to her what passed at that time.

She discovered, however, where his sepulcher

was situated, and resolved to have her share in renewing the flowers that adorned his tomb. But what was her surprise to see among the wreaths and garlands usually placed there a palm branch occupying the most conspicuous place! What right had her father to this distinguishing mark of Christianity? She asked herself this question again and again, and when she reached home she ventured to question Glaucia.

The poor girl colored deeply. The secret of her master's change of faith was one his wife and daughter wished to be buried and forgotten, and Glaucia had not dared to mention it even to one of her fellow-slaves, although she knew that they suspected something of the kind. So now that Claudia came with her questions about this she knew not what to do, for she had no wish to rouse her mistress's anger still more, and she knew if it came to her ears that the matter had been talked of she would be deeply incensed.

Claudia guessed this was why she continued silent, and she said, "Trust me, Glaucia, I will not speak of this matter again. Are we not sisters in Christ, and therefore it behooveth us to help and defend each other. But tell me if thou knowest aught concerning my father, for think what my grief has been fearing that he died without Christ and without hope."

"He did not," answered Glaucia quickly; "forgive me that I did not tell thee this before, but I feared my mistress would be sorely grieved and angry."

"I will not tell Valeria," said the lady, "but thou wilt relate to me now all that passed before my father's death."

Thus pressed, Glaucia told her of the visits of Dionysius, and likewise what had been said concerning the vanity of philosophy.

"And yet my noble sister hopes to find what my father failed to discover in the writings of Plato and Socrates—what I hoped to gain by faithful watch and tendance at the sacred fire of Vesta—rest for the unsatisfied longings of the soul. O, Valeria! I weep to think of thy long, vain, hopeless search, and how the prize is offered thee, and yet is spurned, because it comes not in the way thou expectest to find it."

"The noble Valeria will find it as her father did," said Glaucia gently.

"Thou thinkest so!" said Claudia quickly.

"I have prayed for her," replied Glaucia, with downcast eyes.

Claudia started. "Didst thou ever pray for me?" she asked.

Glaucia's head drooped lower. "I could not help it," she murmured; "thou saidst thou couldst almost believe, and I prayed the Lord Christ that it might not long be almost, but altogether."

Claudia was deeply moved. "I was not worthy of thy prayers," she said, "for I was base and unfaithful, in that I turned away from this faith because of the shame and disgrace that would follow. Thou hast been brave and true, Glaucia, and the Lord hath honored thy faith and courage; but I—it may be I have hindered my sister receiving this truth," she said with a deep sigh.

"Then we will pray the more earnestly that the Lord Christ will himself convince her," said Glaucia hopefully.

It was not often that Glaucia and Claudia had an opportunity of speaking to each other. Valeria seemed to understand that the two young Christians would like to be together—that there now existed a mysterious bond between them stronger than that of blood or kindred, and so to prevent the mutual strength to be obtained from converse together she took care to keep Glaucia employed about her own person as much as possible.

And so the weeks of summer and autumn

slipped away, Valeria growing more and more restless and dissatisfied, and yet returning to the study of the philosophy her father had found so hopeless with redoubled ardor, only to give it up with an aching sense of want and despair, little dreaming that her quiet, unobtrusive waiting-maid was noticing the signs of the struggle going on in her heart.

And so the bleak winter came round again, and the slaves began once more to prepare for the approaching saturnalia, for this feast was one looked forward to with anxious care, and provided for accordingly.

The last days of November had come, and the quiet household of Romola began to stir with something of the bustle to which it was accustomed before her husband's death, when a sudden stop was again put to these preparations by the hasty arrival of a messenger from Rome —a faithful slave of Julia's, who brought not letters from his mistress, but the lady herself, prostrate with illness and quite insane. She had not spoken a sensible word for some days before they left the city, the man said; in fact, it was to that they owed their escape, or she would probably have refused to do so.

"Escape!" repeated Valeria. "What has happened, then?" she asked.

For answer, the man covered his face with his hands and shuddered. "The tidings of Rome being burned hath already reached Athens, I doubt not," he said.

Valeria started. "Rome burned!" she exclaimed; "nay, nay, tell me what it is; we have heard naught concerning such a calamity."

"It is, alas! too true," said the slave. "Half the city hath been destroyed, and it is whispered—nay, it is a well-known fact among many—that the emperor set it on fire with his own hand."

"Nero set his own city on fire!" repeated Valeria in astonishment.

"Yes, not only so, but sat and watched it burning, and played on his lyre the while," said the man.

"And this is known, and Romans bear it?" said Valeria passionately.

"It began to be talked about, and the emperor saw that the Romans would *not* bear it, and so he had to seek for some victim great enough to satiate the popular fury, and at last the despised sect of the Nazarenes were thought of, and the tale was industriously spread that they were guilty of doing this, and they were at once seized, and, almost without the form of a trial, condemned to the most horrible torture."

"And my Julia, having been deluded into joining this miserable sect, hath been made to suffer for this religion," said Valeria.

"Nay, nay; there hath been no accusation brought against her on account of her religion," said the slave; "but I heard it testified that she had with her own hands set fire to one of the houses. In vain I pleaded that I had attended her that night to another part of the city. No one would listen to me, and she was condemned to be burned the second night to illuminate the emperor's garden."

"My Julia be burned—the gentle, loving woman, who ever cared for the sorrows of others more than her own ease—accused of setting fire to a house! Nay, nay; I had rather believe it were the emperor ten times over!" exclaimed Valeria. "But how did she escape? Tell me every thing, for in her present condition it is needful we should know all."

"Nay, nay, I could not tell thee *all*," said the man; "I am not a Christian; but when I saw these people, many of them as good and gentle as my mistress herself, condemned to a hideous death, and compelled to witness friends and relatives put to the most horrible torture, I felt a burning hatred against the religion and the gods who could suffer such things to be done;"

and again the man shuddered at the thought of what he had witnessed.

"And these Christians did not deny their faith to escape the accusation?" asked Valeria.

"Nay, they confessed to being of this sect, but they denied the crime of which they were accused, and many knew they were innocent; but it pleased Nero to turn the popular fury against them, and provide himself with another illumination. It was this that turned my mistress's brain, and, doubtless, many others besides—the being compelled to witness friends rolled in garments soaked with pitch, and then chained to posts and set on fire to illuminate the emperor's gardens at night.

"O, hush! hush!" exclaimed Valeria. "My poor Julia," what she must have suffered!"

"She was condemned to the same suffering, was being carried to the place where the pitched garments were lying in readiness, when I volunteered to take the place of one who was suddenly called away, and in the hurry and confusion I threw a toga I had with me over her shoulders, and, by the help of one of the guards whom she had befriended, we passed through unquestioned, and I at once took ship for Athens, for Drusilla had told me of her visit here, and moreover, being a Jewess, she was less likely to be suspected of holding a faith which the Jews hate so much."

"Thou hast done well to bear her hither," said Valeria; "and now, since it will not be safe for thee to return to Rome, I will consult with my mother about sending our freedman, Anicetus, to secure some part of her wealth, for she will have to remain in Athens now."

Romola remembered what she had said before leaving Rome, when Julia was carried to the room hastily prepared for her reception, and she was glad the invitation had been given, and that her slaves knew of it, although it might bring some trouble and inconvenience if the prefect heard that they were concealing one who had been condemned by the emperor.

This danger was mentioned both to Drusilla and the slave, and they were warned not to talk of the matter to any one; a warning scarcely needed, since both shrank with horror from recalling that hideous, appalling spectacle; for Drusilla, although she could not see, had been compelled to hear shrieks and groans, while hovering round her mistress's prison, that would resound in her ears until her dying day.

In the new interest of nursing Julia, Valeria seemed to forget her anger against her sister and Glaucia; for her condition was so critical, and the physicians ordered so much care and quiet, that no slave but Drusilla was allowed to enter her chamber, lest she should answer the questions Julia was continually putting to her nurses in such a way as to recall the scenes they were so anxious to obliterate from her mind.

Valeria proved a more skillful nurse than her mother, and the patient was more quiet and composed while Valeria sat by her bedside, and one day asked her to read in a voice so rational that she thought she must have recovered her reason, only that the reading she asked for was such as she knew nothing of, although she judged truly enough that it concerned the Christian faith, and could be obtained of Dionysius, even if Drusilla had not secured it among the manuscripts that she knew she had brought with her.

The next day, when Valeria was again sitting by her, she repeated her request, and the lady resolved to gratify it if possible, for since hearing of this terrible persecution against these people she felt some curiosity to read some of their writings. Perhaps the curiosity existed before, and needed very little to rouse it; for, however she tried to forget it or blind herself to the fact, she *knew* that her father had embraced this despised faith before his death. She remembered, too, the charge he had once given her, never to give up her search for light until she found it, in whatever direction it might lead her; and she had heard from him, and from Julia, too, that this religion alone brought "life and immortality to light." So Drusilla was asked for the casket containing her mistress's parchments, and from two or three small rolls Valeria took one and sat down to read it aloud. It was the Sermon on the Mount, and before she had read far Valeria became convinced that it was no ordinary man who could utter such words, and she read on with earnest attention and increasing interest, quite oblivious of the fact that the words, so strange to her but so familiar to the invalid, had brought back memories of other times, and so soothed and refreshed her weary spirit that she had fallen into a sleep so quiet and natural that Valeria had well-nigh forgotten her presence even, until she came to the close of the manuscript.

"Truly this seemeth to be as a healing medicine to thy mistress," she said as she saw Drusilla keeping her faithful watch at the foot of the bed.

"If my mistress could only hear and receive once more these gracious words it would heal her troubled mind," said Drusilla with a sigh.

"Then thou thinkest I should read to her every day," said Valeria with a slight start as she saw her sister enter the room, while she still held the manuscript in her hand.

Claudia noticed the heightened color in her sister's cheeks, and then saw that she had been reading what Julia had often read to her, but she felt afraid to speak of this now. Whenever she felt inclined to mention her change of faith, there came to her remembrance that time when she had so basely stifled her convictions and declared that she was Claudia the vestal still, when she knew she ought to have said that all faith in these old superstitions had gone forever. Had she done this, and firmly declared her faith in Christ to her father, he might have received the Gospel from her lips, and Valeria as well; but now this honor was taken from her, and, as an unworthy servant, she must stand aside and let others do the glorious work that might and ought of right to be hers.

These were her thoughts as she stood and looked at Julia and her sister; but when she heard Valeria ask Drusilla to hand the casket of manuscripts over to her care, and saw her take them to her own room, she lifted her heart in praise to God that he had not rejected her prayer.

An hour or two later there was a little gathering in Claudia's room, for she sent for Glaucia to tell her the joyful news that Valeria had begun to study the words of the Lord Christ, and they both, with Drusilla, kneeled to pray that the Holy Spirit might be given to enlighten her, that she, too, might give her heart to Christ and cast in her lot with his people.

CHAPTER XXII.

CONCLUSION.

THE news brought by Julia's slave of the cruel persecution of the Christians in Rome was made known to the little Church at Athens, and they resolved to send the warning to their brethren at Corinth, for it might be they had not yet heard of it, though what they would do in the matter they could not tell. Certainly they would not forsake their God if this offer should be made them as a means of escape.

Laon had so approved himself to the members of the Church that, now a trusty messenger was wanted who could journey to Corinth with speed and discretion, he was unanimously chosen for the business of carrying letters from Dionysius and the presbyters to the angel and presbyters of the Corinthian congregation, which was a very dangerous act now.

Arnobius was greatly pleased that his young favorite had been chosen for the difficult duty, and readily agreed to dispense with his services in the market, although he was so useful now, and had made himself so popular with the customers by his kindness and readiness to oblige that his business had increased very much, and it would be difficult to carry it on by himself.

Lepida, however, strongly opposed this undertaking, and talked of the dangers of such a journey, and Laon's unfitness for it, until both he and Arnobius began to think she must have some ulterior motive for wishing him to refuse it. This, however, he was not likely to do, for her present unwillingness for him to go to Corinth brought to his mind several things connected with her visit there, and he resolved to make some inquiries about his mother when he delivered the letters of the Church.

There was little need to urge him to secresy or dispatch. As soon as the papyrus-rolls were written and sealed he was ready to set off with them, in spite of the light flakes of snow that were gently descending as he passed through the gate of the city. It was not often that snow was seen in Athens, and the people thought no one should be abroad when it did fall, so it was not likely he would meet many passengers during his forty-five-mile walk; but this would save him from the inconvenience of answering questions he might be troubled with, and the loneliness he did not mind, for he had one important matter to settle—how he should begin his inquiries for his mother. The letters to the Church must be delivered first, and then he would cautiously put some questions to some of the people he met, or call upon the deaconess, Phœbe, who had sent the money for Glaucia's redemption, and tell her some portion of his story and ask her help to enable him to find his mother.

This last plan seemed the best he could adopt; and when at length he reached Corinth, weary and footsore, after his two days' march, he went to the house of the minister, and, after delivering the letters, asked for Phœbe the deaconess.

"Nay; but tarry awhile and rest and refresh thyself while I break these seals," said the minister as he heard the inquiry; "unless thou art the bearer of tidings to our sister," he added.

"Nay; but I would fain hear tidings of one who came to Corinth, as I believe, many years ago, and hath not been to Athens since," said Laon.

The minister looked at Laon very earnestly. "Thou art in search of one who formerly lived at Athens," he said; "tarry until I have read these letters, and then I will talk further upon this matter;" and he carried the papyrus-rolls into his own private room, for he knew not what important news they might contain.

Laon sat down in the undecorated atrium to wait, but he had not been there two minutes when the curtain was drawn from the entrance, and two plainly-dressed ladies entered. One of them started as her eyes fell upon Laon, and she stood still with heaving breast, and a face from which it seemed the eyes would start in the intensity of her gaze.

"What is it moves my sister?" asked her companion, noticing her emotion; while, by some strange, far-off remembrance or fascination, Laon never raised his eyes from her face.

For a minute or two they stood thus looking at each other, and then in a quick, panting whisper came the words, "It is—it must be my Laon!"

For answer, Laon stumbled forward and caught the reeling figure.

"My mother!" he gasped, and the two were locked in an embrace so passionate, so long, that Phœbe feared for her friend's over-taxed powers, and, gently touching Laon's shoulder, she said,

"Be careful—she is not strong."

He needed no second hint. Mastering his emotion, he partly led, partly carried his mother to a couch close at hand, and, gently placing her upon it, kneeled down to look at the face from which every particle of color had faded, while Phœbe went in search of some restorative. The minister's wife, a gentle matron, came in, bringing a cup of spiced wine, and handed it to Laon, who pressed his mother to drink a little before she attempted to speak again.

She managed to swallow a little, and then whispered, "You are faint, my son, you need it;" and then from his face her eyes wandered to the peasant's garment he wore, travel-stained and dusty, and she seemed to ask some explanation of this.

But Laon saw it would not be wise to tell her too much of his story until she was better. Drinking some of the wine, he said, "I am weary; I have traveled many miles to-day, my mother."

"Thou hast escaped from Rome as best thou couldst," said the lady; "but—but my little Glaucia," she whispered.

"Glaucia is safe, my mother," said Laon; "she is in Athens."

For a minute or two the mother lay with closed eyes, while a radiant smile beamed over her face, and, turning toward Phœbe, she said, "Did I not tell thee that God would bring my children to my arms again?" Then, looking at Laon, she said, "But, my son, how knewest thou where to search for me?"

"I truly came in search of thee, for I judged thou must be in Corinth from what Lepida once said; but I also came as a messenger from the Church of Athens, to bring tidings of the persecution of the Christians in Rome."

"Thou camest from the Church at Athens?" said Hyrmina, passing her hand over her forehead, as if her senses were growing confused. "Dost thou know the Christian Church at Athens?" she asked.

"I am a Christian; I am a member of the Athenian Church," said Laon.

A look of almost ineffable joy, that was too great to find utterance in words, for a few minutes shone in her tearful eyes; but at last she managed to whisper, "And my Glaucia!"

Laon understood the question. "Glaucia is a Christian too—the noblest Christian in Athens," he added warmly.

"It is enough. Phœbe, my sister, praise God for me or I shall die before I can give thanks;" and indeed it seemed as though the overwhelming joy would prove too much for her feeble strength, and a physician had to be sent for immediately.

As yet Hyrmina did not know of her daughter's condition; but as Dionysius again failed to induce Valeria to release her, and Hyrmina began to grow stronger, they resolved to tell her the full reason why she could not leave Athens —that it was not alone the difficulty of traveling that prevented Glaucia from coming to her bedside, but because she was a slave.

"My—Glaucia—a—slave—in—Athens!" she repeated slowly; "was it to her, then, that my heart was strongly drawn in sympathy when Julia visited us last year!"

"Yes, it was thy daughter thou so earnestly tried to release, although we little knew it at that time," said Phœbe.

"And I must try again," said Hyrmina. "This Roman lady, hard as she may be, cannot resist a mother's prayers. The Lord Christ will plead with her for me—I will go to Athens and redeem my child."

No one attempted to dissuade her, for it seemed the only way by which Glaucia could be released, and from this time it was marvelous to notice how rapidly she regained health and strength. In a few weeks she was able to undertake the journey, and, accompanied by Laon, she set off for Athens, Dionysius having offered to entertain her while there.

Laon stopped to see Lepida and inform her of all that had happened, quite expecting she would be very angry when she heard it. But, to his surprise, she met him with such a pale, weary, anxious face, that he asked if she had been ill.

"Nay, nay, not ill, but unhappy, wretched, and miserable. But how is my noble mistress, thy mother?" she asked anxiously.

"Better," answered Laon; and he could not help adding, "O, Lepida, why didst thou not tell me where to find my mother before?"

"Because thy father made me swear by the gods that I would ever try to keep thee from her. I tried to keep my oath even when I broke it by giving thee those parchments, and now the gods have forsaken me, and I am friendless and alone in the world."

"Nay, nay, my mother will be thy friend," said Laon, "and thou shalt learn to love our God and Saviour, and then thou wilt be happy with Arnobius again," he added in a whisper.

She did not repulse him, or refuse the comfort he tried to give her; but she shook her head sadly as she said, "I am not worthy to look in thy mother's face again; and thy God would surely reject an old woman who has given the best of her days to the service of those thou callest idols."

Laon could not stay long, for his mother's litter had passed and he was anxious to overtake it; but he whispered as he bade her farewell, "My mother will forgive thee, and the Lord Christ will receive thee," and then he turned his horse's head once more toward Athens, and rode after his mother.

As soon as they reached the house of Dionysius Hyrmina alighted, and securing a change of bearers for her litter, she only stayed long enough to put on a costly tunic and robe, such as she wore in the old days before her banishment, and then she went on at once to present herself before Valeria.

She sent a message by the slave to say that Hyrmina, a noble Athenian matron, desired to see Valeria, the Roman maiden. The man was evidently impressed by the gentle majesty of her bearing, and ushered her into the atrium at once, and sent a message to his mistress.

Valeria was reading to Julia, who was slowly regaining her health and reason too, but was too weak to be left to the care of slaves entirely. She looked annoyed when this visitor was announced, and sent Drusilla in search of Glaucia to take a message of excuse; but Glaucia was not to be found, and so the lady was obliged to lay aside her reading to go and see her visitor.

She was evidently impressed when she saw Hyrmina, and received her with a lowly reverence as her equal in rank but superior in years; but what was her astonishment to see the tall, stately, elegantly dressed lady fall on her knees, and with clasped hands implore her to give her back her child.

"Thy child!" repeated Valeria, looking down at the agonized face, and thinking that she, too, must be insane. Fearing this was certainly her condition, she was about to summon Anicetus and some of the slaves, when Glaucia stepped out of the alcove leading to Claudia's room.

"My Glaucia! my child! my long lost daughter!" exclaimed the kneeling suppliant, rushing toward the girl and clasping her in her arms. For a minute or two mother and child were clasped in a fond embrace; but Hyrmina was the first to recover herself, and remember she was in Valeria's presence.

"Kneel with me, Glaucia, and pray thy mistress to suffer me to ransom thee," she said, again falling on her knees at Valeria's feet. "I care not what sum thou dost ask," she said, appealing again to the lady; "I am rich, and my children are of noble birth."

"Rich and of noble birth," repeated Valeria.

"Dost thou know, then, that Glaucia has disgraced thee, and calls herself a Christian?"

Hyrmina lifted her head and looked at Valeria. "I, too, am a Christian," she said; "for this I had to give up husband, children, kindred, and country, for twelve years, since I was banished from Athens, because I would not deny my Master; and thinkest thou it is a disgrace to be called by the sacred name of Christ, who is King of kings and Lord of lords! Nay, nay; it is the highest honor to which we can aspire, and I would rather have my daughter what she is, a Christian slave, than an idolatrous queen."

"Glaucia is no longer a slave," said Valeria as soon as she could recover from her astonishment sufficiently to speak; "when her mother claims her she is free. Nay, nay, rise to thy feet," she said as Hyrmina bent in lowly thanks before her; "I knew not that thou didst claim her before," she added.

Glaucia herself was in such a state of joyful bewilderment that she knew not what to do, until her mother took her hand to lead her to her litter. Then she remembered Claudia and Drusilla, and ran to tell them what had happened.

"Glaucia, God hath heard thy prayer, and

thou wilt join his Church ; will it be answered likewise for Valeria ?"

A few months later that question was answered. Glaucia and Laon had gone to Corinth with their mother ; but most of the other actors in this story were gathered in a large, plainly-furnished hall outside the gates of Athens. This was a special gathering of the Athenian Church, and they had met to receive two new converts from idolatry. There were nearly forty people assembled, sitting in a semicircle, with their minister, Dionysius, in the midst. Each were silently praying for the presence and help of God's Holy Spirit, when the door opened and Arnobius entered, leading his wife by the hand, and immediately behind him came the old preacher leading Valeria.

"Men and brethren," he said, advancing to the front, between the two candidates, "these who once were blind hath the Spirit of God enlightened, and given them the desire to join us, that they may see, and know, and understand more of his truth."

"Let them come," said each in turn, Julia and Claudia being of the number, and then they were led to the seat occupied by the catechumens.

A prayer and lecture followed, after which

some little children were led in and placed before Dionysius, who exhorted them in language suitable to their age. Then, after blessing them, he turned to the rest of the congregation and said, "Except ye be converted, and become as little children, ye shall not enter into the kingdom of heaven."

THE END.

www.ingramcontent.com/pod-product-compliance
Lightning Source LLC
LaVergne TN
LVHW020238110826
845151LV00003B/957

* 9 7 8 1 4 2 5 5 3 0 2 4 2 *